Jason dropped the shell and took her hand. "Hilary, you've *got* to depend on other people—that's part of being human." He stood up and brushed the sand off his trunks. "Come on, let's pack up your painting gear. I've got something to show you."

They walked single file for almost a mile back up into the dunes. They didn't talk, and Hilary was glad. There was too much going on inside her head, and she wasn't sure she could trust herself to speak.

Jason had followed her up the beach; he'd said he wanted to be friends. What did he mean? Could he possibly mean—? Hilary shook her head in disbelief. No, he just meant *friends*, that was all.

But she could still feel the warmth and strength of his fingers around hers, and her heart beat faster as she followed him through the dunes.

A Change of Heart

Susan Blake

BANTAM BOOKS

TORONTO · NEW YORK · LONDON · SYDNEY · AUCKLAND

RL 7, IL age 11 and up

A CHANGE OF HEART
A Bantam Book/November 1986

Cover photograph by Pat Hill.

ISBN 0-553-26168-1

Published simultaneously in the United States and Canada

Bantam Books are published by Bantam Books, Inc. Its trademark, consisting of the words "Bantam Books" and the por-
trayal of a rooster, is Registered in U.S. Patent and Trademark
Office and in other countries. Marca Registrada. Bantam
Books, Inc., 666 Fifth Avenue, New York, New York 10103.

Printed and bound in Great Britain by
Cox & Wyman Ltd., Reading

O   0 9 8 7 6 5 4 3 2 1

For Michael George,
who shared the beach with me

Chapter One

The first thing Hilary Malone did when she got to the top of the dune was to sit down and pull off her sneakers. Even though the early-summer sun was dropping swiftly toward the horizon, the sand still felt warm as she curled her bare toes into it. Behind her the eastern sky over the Gulf of Mexico was gradually darkening. Before her, toward the west, stretched the unruffled water of the Laguna Madre, the slender, fingerlike bay that separated Padre Island from the Texas mainland nearly eight miles away. Above the lagoon the sunset sky was a soft pink, like the rosy inside of the conch shell that sat on Hilary's bedroom shelf in the beach house she shared with her mother and her nineteen-year-old sister, Amy.

1

Hilary frowned at her easel and water-color box, which were leaning against a clump of brown grass next to her. She knew that she ought to get to work quickly if she was going to paint that night's sunset as she had planned. But thinking about Amy had reminded her of their most recent argument and of how angry she still felt. There was no point trying to paint when she was in a dark mood. Everything would probably turn out an ugly purple—just the color she felt inside!

A miniature crab with brown stripes scut-tled sideways across the dune, stopping about an inch from Hilary's bare foot, but she scarcely saw it. Her mind was on the argu-ment. This time, she and her sister had fought over something even more trivial than usual. All she had done was to track a little bit of sand onto the pink rug in Amy's bedroom. But Amy had gotten really angry. "I've told you over and over not to track sand in here!" she had said between clenched teeth. "I've just run the vacuum cleaner, and now I'll have to do it all over again! You've got your own room—stay out of mine!"

Amy was dainty and sweet-looking, but when she got angry, her big eyes narrowed, and her soft voice turned shrill. These days, it seemed to Hilary, Amy got angry over every-thing. There was no getting around the fact that things weren't right between Amy and her. The two of them hadn't really been close since their parents' separation a year and a half before.

Of course, Hilary thought, she and Amy had always been very different, and people sometimes had trouble believing they really were sisters. Amy had inherited their mother's delicate prettiness, with a heart-shaped face, ash-blond hair, and deep blue eyes. She was very fragile-looking, almost like a Victorian doll, and people had a tendency to treat her as though she might break.

Hilary, on the other hand, resembled her father—a fact that she resented every time she looked in the mirror. Like him she was tall, taller than many of the boys in her class, with a sprinkling of freckles across her nose and thick, reddish-brown hair, which tumbled down around her shoulders, despite Amy's hints that it would look prettier trimmed. She was much more athletically inclined than Amy, whose interest in sports stopped with cheerleading. Being athletic hadn't done a great deal for her popularity, Hilary decided. Boys seemed to like fragile-looking, non-athletic girls like Amy.

Hilary often thought that the only really *useful* thing she had inherited from her father was his eyes. They were bright green and

3

slightly upturned at the corners, with thick copper lashes. "Leprechaun's eyes," her dad used to say. They were definitely her best feature, Hilary thought.

She couldn't help being a little bit jealous of Amy's looks and of how popular she had been at Port Isabel High, on the mainland, where Hilary now went to school. Amy was a hard act to follow. She seemed to find it easy to laugh and tease and flirt, and her casual friendliness had brought her lots of friends. Hilary had only two really good girlfriends, who would be working the entire summer on the mainland where they lived. She would be practically friendless the entire summer.

Also, Amy had started dating when she was fifteen—a year younger than Hilary was now, as Amy often pointed out. And, she had dated a lot of different boys until she started going with Brad right after her high-school graduation a year ago. Secretly Hilary had looked forward to Amy's graduation, thinking that her sister would be going away to college in the fall. But it hadn't worked out that way because, much to Hilary's dismay, at the last minute Amy had decided to stay home, work part-time, and go to a junior college on the mainland.

"What's wrong with me? What's wrong with *us*?" Hilary demanded out loud. "Amy is my only sister, for pete's sake. Why can't we get along like we used to?"

Sighing, Hilary stood up and slapped the sand off her shorts. If thinking about Amy made her angry, thinking about her father's absence made her furious. Amy had always been closer to their mother, but ever since Hilary was little, she had been her father's girl. When he had left she felt deserted and unloved. He hadn't gone that far—Houston was only about three hundred and fifty miles north—but he had his own life there. And it must be a very busy life, Hilary had decided, because he didn't write or come to visit very often. The few times he had come, things were awkward and strained between them. The old, easy companionship was gone, and Hilary missed it terribly.

Hilary tried to push the resentment she felt for her father out of her mind. If she were going to paint that night, she'd have to get started before the sun dropped too low. She snapped open the small folding easel and set the legs of the tripod firmly against the steep slant of the dune. Then she pinned her half-finished watercolor to the easel. She had already applied a blue-gray wash to the upper third of the painting and a deeper cobalt blue to the lower two-thirds, with a wedge of dark brown to represent the tidal flats. Now she needed to capture the sunset swirl of pink and lavender clouds.

Hilary had been painting for years, but she was just beginning to believe that she might have some talent. "Your painting is really coming along, Hilary," Elena Morrison had said approvingly when Hilary had shown her a recent watercolor of a fishing pier. "If you keep on painting like this, there's a good chance we'll be hanging your work in the gallery before summer vacation is over."

Elena was Mrs. Malone's friend and her partner in a gallery and art supply shop called the White Pelican, which the two of them had opened in the village of South Padre.

Elena had an ability to spot undiscovered artistic talent and show it off to great advantage, and buyers from as far away as Dallas came to the gallery. Hilary felt really encouraged by Elena's interest, and it made her want to try even harder to produce something good.

Now, as she looked out across the lagoon, Hilary saw a long-legged egret stalking fish in the shallows, its feathers a splash of brilliant white against the rosy pink of the sunset, and she decided to use the bird to give the scene more dimension. She opened her watercolor box and started to work. But after ten minutes she put her brush down and stepped back, regarding her work dejectedly. Her shoulders slumped. It wasn't right. She wasn't sure why, but it wasn't right.

"Actually, it's not as bad as you seem to think."

Startled, Hilary turned swiftly, caught her foot in a clump of dune grass, and sat down abruptly in the sand, dropping her brush. The speaker was Jason Wolf, who Hilary knew from Port Isabel High. A tall boy, taller than she, with rather long, dark hair and penetrating blue eyes, he had a camera on a leather strap around his neck. He looked at her quizzically and held out his hand to help her up. "Do you always fall down when somebody says something nice about your work, Hilary?"

"I do when that somebody is rude enough to sneak up behind me and scare me," Hilary retorted. She ignored Jason's outstretched hand and struggled clumsily to her feet.

"I'm sorry," Jason said. His smile was gone, and his blue eyes had darkened. "I was just thinking out loud. I didn't mean to startle you." He looked again at the easel. "I guess I was remembering the watercolor you did in your art class this spring—the one of the tidal flats with the brown pelicans perched on the pilings. I liked it a lot. I was wondering if you were going to do something like that again, with this painting."

Hilary looked at him in surprise. The art

teacher *had* put up her painting, but it was one of about fifty student works on display. "You remember *my* watercolor?" she asked.

Jason was one of the most popular and good-looking boys in school. For the last couple of years, he had been going with an equally popular girl, a cute, petite, blond cheerleader named Cindy Morris. But what made him stand out in Hilary's mind was that he was the very best artist at Port Isabel High. He had won half a dozen prizes for his work, mostly oil paintings, and she had admired the crisp, clean lines of his paintings, which were also in the school exhibit. Hilary was flabbergasted that Jason Wolf even knew her name, let alone her painting.

"Well, sure I remember," Jason said, and Hilary noticed that his voice was deeper and richer than she had recalled. "You've got a low-key style, not very flashy, but there's something about your work that makes it hard to forget." He was looking at her with a half smile, and there was an amused glint in his blue eyes. Hilary was suddenly aware of her breeze-tangled hair and sandy shorts.

She turned away, blushing. For some reason, the way Jason was looking at her made her feel uncomfortable, even though she couldn't help being pleased that he had remembered her work. "How long have you been standing back there, spying on me?" she demanded.

"I wasn't spying," Jason replied evenly. "My parents and I moved over to the island from Port Isabel after school let out. Dad's managing the Jetties, that big complex south of the village, so it's easier for him if we live over here." He smiled. "I'm glad we moved. I love the dunes, and I've been spending a lot of time here. I was taking pictures when I spotted you here painting. I thought I'd come over and see what you were doing."

"Well, now you've seen it," Hilary said. She retrieved her brush and wiped the grit off it. "The sun will be gone pretty soon, and I'd like to finish this watercolor tonight." She turned back to her painting, expecting Jason to walk away.

But he didn't. He just stood there, looking over her shoulder while she worked, terribly conscious of his presence.

"I meant what I said a minute ago," he said after a while. "Your painting is really pretty good. I like it a lot. There's just one thing about your technique—" He paused as if expecting Hilary to say something.

The silence deepened. Finally, Hilary lowered her brush. "All right," she said. "What *is* it?" After all, she hadn't been able to figure out what was wrong. Maybe Jason could tell her something that would help.

Jason moved close behind her, and Hilary stiffened at his nearness. "You're working way too slowly, and you're paying too much attention to details. You can always add the small stuff later, when you've got the major shapes blocked." He pointed at a corner of the watercolor. "For example, you spent nearly five minutes shading this area of the beach, but you haven't defined the whole shape yet."

Hilary stepped aside, interested in spite of herself. "Well, what do you suggest?" she asked shortly.

"At this stage, I'd say you need to work faster, to aim for a swift impression rather than a detail-by-detail reproduction of the landscape." Jason looked down at her, and Hilary noticed again how tall he was. Her head only came up to his shoulder. "After all, a watercolor isn't a photograph," he continued, and Hilary forced her attention back to the painting. "Here, let me show you."

Jason took the brush from her fingers and wet it slightly, turning to a section of the sky. "Fast strokes, loose wrist," he muttered as if repeating a teacher's instruction. "Make it simple, dash it off, and your painting will look less cramped. You could work with a drier

brush, too. That will give you a more sponta-
neous feel."

Hilary watched, fascinated by Jason's move-
ments. His swift brush strokes had a free,
easy rhythm, and the clouds that took shape
had mass and depth and a soft, delicate color.
After a minute he stepped back and handed
her the brush. "There," he said with satisfaction. "Loosen up a little. Don't be so tense
and uptight. I'm sure you'll see a big
improvement."

Loosen up! That was the expression Amy
used when she was nagging her about being
more friendly around guys. Why couldn't people leave her alone? Hilary's anger flared up
uncontrollably. "You can keep your advice to
yourself, Jason Wolf," she snapped, pulling
the watercolor from the easel and ripping it
violently in half. "I didn't ask for it, and I don't
need it." Without looking at him, she dumped
her brushes into her watercolor tray and
closed it with a snap.

"I wish you hadn't done that, Hilary," Jason
said, regarding her with a puzzled look. He
picked up the two pieces of the watercolor and
held them together, squinting at them. "It was
a good piece—or it *could* have been, with a little more work."

"But it wasn't *my* work," Hilary retorted.
"Why is it that everyone wants to improve on

11

me?" She was thinking of Amy again, and in her anger she folded up the legs of the easel too quickly and pinched her finger in the hinge. The pain brought tears to her eyes. Instinctively she put her finger in her mouth and began to suck on it.

Jason took the easel, finished folding it up, and handed it back to her. "I really didn't mean—"

"Never mind," Hilary said, feeling embarrassed about her outburst. She tucked her color box and easel under her arm. "I have to go now."

Jason was looking at her with an odd expression on his face. "You know, Hilary," he said suddenly, "I think I'd like to do a portrait of you. Would you pose for me?"

"No," she said abruptly. Seeing Jason Wolf again was the *last* thing Hilary wanted. She turned and started down the dune, slipping slightly in the sand.

"Hey, wait," Jason called when she was halfway down. He was waving something. "Your sneakers."

Face burning, Hilary climbed back through the loose sand to the top of the dune. "Thanks," she muttered. She bent over and pulled her shoes on, not bothering to tie the laces.

"That's OK," Jason said. "See you later."

Hilary clambered back down the dune. At the bottom she tripped on her untied laces and fell, dropping her color box.

"Need some help?" Jason called.

Hilary ignored him. But she could feel his eyes on her, almost like a physical touch, as she walked back across the beach toward her home.

Chapter Two

Today was a good day, Hilary thought with satisfaction as she walked home the next afternoon. She had spent several hours on the dunes, making pencil studies and small, quick sketches of the sea oat grasses and wild morning glories that clung stubbornly to the cliffs and helped hold them against the constantly shifting winds. Much as she hated to admit it, Jason's suggestion the evening before—that she work faster, not trying for as much detail—had been a good one. She could see the difference in the work she had done that day, and she was sorry that she'd torn up the watercolor.

The afternoon was overcast, and the low line of dark clouds that rimmed the lagoon to the west promised rain before sunset. Ahead, down the narrow, sandy road was the Malones' house. Hilary and her family had lived on Padre Island, just outside the village of South Padre, ever since she could remember. The island, which was more than eighty miles long and only about five miles across at its widest point, lay along the north-south curve of the Texas coast, just north of the Mexican border. It was linked to the mainland by a long, narrow concrete-and-steel causeway that spanned the lagoon.

Tourists, and lots of them, came to spend the winter. That was the part that Hilary liked least. When it was snowing and icy up north, the "snowbirds," as the local people called the tourists, migrated to the island in huge, noisy flocks to enjoy the warm winter sunshine and the sea breezes. For the last few years many of the tourists had even started coming in the summer, so that what had once been a quiet fishing village at the south end of the island was now a cluster of high-rise hotels, fancy shops, and expensive condominiums that were busy year-round.

As far as Hilary was concerned, the tourists could do whatever they pleased with *their* end of the island, as long as they left the dunes at the northern end alone. And most of them did because the paved highway took them only a few miles north, up the middle of the island, and generally they didn't like to walk very far from their cars. To Hilary, the most beautiful places on the island were even farther north, hidden away in the dunes where no one ever went. They were places where the evening primrose bloomed fragrant against gnarled gray roots; where the cool salt breeze drifted heaps of sand into symmetrical shapes, embroidered with the looping stitchery of sand crab and snail tracks; and where she could sit alone for hours, disturbed only by dragonflies with wonderful fairylike wings that shone iridescent in the sun.

In those places Hilary felt as if she were a part of the world of the dunes—not an intruder from the outside, but somebody who was welcomed by the dragonflies and the sand crabs and even the noisy gulls. It was a feeling she wished she could capture in her paintings.

The Malone house was only about fifty yards from the lagoon. Like many of the other homes on the island, it stood on heavy wooden stilts, out of reach of the high tides that sometimes accompanied Gulf storms. It was surrounded on all four sides by a raised redwood deck, weathered a soft silvery gray.

That day as she walked up the drive that led to the house, she noticed that the family station wagon was gone from its usual parking place beside the stairs leading to the deck. That must mean that her mother and Amy weren't back from their shopping trip to the mainland. Brad had invited Amy to a dance the next week at the yacht club, where Amy worked as a waitress. She had insisted that she couldn't find anything to wear in any of the island shops.

Hilary smiled ruefully. At the rate she was going, it wasn't likely that *she* would ever have an invitation to a yacht club dance. But it didn't really matter. At least she wouldn't have to squeeze her feet into narrow high heels or try to find an evening dress that would fit. Hilary couldn't help giggling at the thought of herself in high heels and a slinky dress, towering over her partner. Oddly, the thought of Jason flashed through her mind. If she went dancing with him, *he'd* be the tall one. She shook her head, frowning. Dancing with Jason Wolf! Where in the world had *that* thought come from? She must be out of her mind!

A white envelope in the mailbox at the foot of the stairs caught her attention. It was a letter from her father, addressed to her and Amy. At the sight of the familiar handwriting, a lump rose in her throat, and she swallowed hard. She thrust the letter, unopened, into the back pocket of her jeans and climbed the stairs without hurrying. She went into the kitchen to get a glass of iced tea and some cookies. She would read the letter in her room.

Hilary's room was small, just large enough for her bed, a dresser, chair and a stand for her stereo, and Hilary had to keep it relatively neat in order to move around comfortably. Amy's room was larger, but Hilary wouldn't have traded for anything because her own room overlooked the lagoon, and Amy's didn't.

The window was the thing that Hilary loved most about her room. It was a wide, tall, casement window that opened out with a crank, giving her a view of water and sky. Underneath was a window seat, and beside it stood her easel. Next to the easel was a little cabinet her father had built for her paints and watercolors. One wall of the room was covered with her paintings and sketches, taped almost to the ceiling. Hilary loved to study them to see how her style had changed over the years she had been painting.

The casement window was open now, and a cool breeze swept through the room, causing the white curtains on either side of the window to billow out. Missy, Hilary's gray- and black-striped cat, was asleep on the window seat. Hilary sat down next to her. "Wake up,

Missy," she said, tugging at the cat's paw. "We've got a letter from Dad."

Missy looked up and blinked, then went back to sleep. Hilary put the envelope on the windowsill and stared at it thoughtfully while she finished her iced tea and cookies. Letters from her dad weren't all that frequent, and getting one, Hilary had to admit, was almost as painful as seeing him. They never failed to stir up a crazy mixture of feelings in her. How could she still love her father when he'd just suddenly gone away, without telling her that he was leaving or letting her know why?

Even though Hilary had thought about it for months, she couldn't remember anything unusual in the weeks before he'd left—or at least nothing that was serious enough to explain what had happened. He had seemed to enjoy his work at the Port Isabel newspaper, and he and her mom hadn't argued all that much. Oh, there had been a few disagreements, mostly about the fact that he had wanted to spend more time doing free-lance writing, which would mean he'd have less time with the family. But the arguments hadn't seemed very important—until the day that he simply left.

Her mom was terribly hurt—you could see it in her eyes—but she had Amy for comfort, and the two of them grew even closer after he had left. Hilary didn't have anyone, and for weeks she had struggled with a bitter anger that almost consumed her. But in spite of the bitterness, she still loved her father. She put down her glass and opened the envelope.

The letter was brief, and when Hilary finished it, she sat still for a long time, gazing out at the dark thunderclouds that now covered half the western sky. Her dad had written about the new book he had just signed a contract to write and about the series of articles he'd decided to do on Houston business. There was also a detailed description of his last trip to San Francisco.

Her dad's life seemed to be full of exciting new experiences, Hilary reflected, very different from the quiet life of the island. But he rarely wrote about what he was thinking or how he was feeling. "Miss you," he had written at the bottom of the second page. "Think of you often." Did he really think about her? Or was it just something that people always put at the end of letters?

"Hello, Hilary, are you home?" her mother called.

Hilary got up quickly, startling Missy, and went into the hallway.

"I'm here," she called. Then, after a pause, she added, "We got a letter from Dad, Amy."

"Terrific!" Amy appeared, carrying a

brightly colored plastic shopping bag. "Let me have it! What's he been doing? Is he coming to see us soon?"

Reluctantly Hilary held out the letter. It was addressed to both of them, but somehow she always felt that her father's letters were more for her than her sister. "He doesn't say so," she said slowly. "He just says he misses us."

"Hmmpf," Amy said, making a face. "He *always* says that. Well, if there's nothing special in it, I'll read it later." She smiled excitedly and tossed her blond ponytail. "Come into my room, Hilary, and watch me try on my new dress—it's really beautiful! And I've got a new pair of shoes to match."

Amy's room was very different from Hilary's. It had pink-flowered wallpaper and pink curtains, and everything, even the lampshade and the mirror, was trimmed with the lace ruffles that Amy loved. It was cute and feminine and suited Amy perfectly. But all that pink and ruffles made Hilary feel claustrophobic.

Amy had dumped the contents of her bag on the bed and was tearing a dress box open. "It's blue and ruffly," she said as Hilary came in, "with little spaghetti straps and a velvet belt." Quickly she pulled off her jeans and blouse and slipped into the dress. "How do you like it?" she asked, twirling in front of the mirror

21

so that the full skirt stood out. "Isn't it *glamorous*?"

Hilary looked at the dress. She had to admit that it *was* pretty. The deep blue of the chiffon made Amy's eyes seem even bluer and showed off her rich tan. "It's very nice," Hilary said.

Amy pouted. "*Nice*? Is that all you can say? Just *nice*?" She raised her arms above her head and struck a pose, admiring herself in the mirror. "It's beautiful—that's all there is to it. It's the most marvelous dress in the whole world!" She went to the bed and opened another box. "And here are the shoes to match. Aren't they simply terrific?"

Suddenly there was an earsplitting roar on the road leading to the house. "Oh, it's Brad!" Amy exclaimed, dropping the shoes. "I don't want him to see me in the dress." She gave Hilary a cajoling smile. "Be a sweetie, and tell him I'll be down in a minute."

Obediently Hilary went down the hall and out onto the deck. Below, in the driveway, Brad was just climbing out of a bright yellow dune buggy. It had thick, heavy tires, flared fenders, and chrome roll bars. The engine didn't have a cover, and from that angle it looked big and powerful. The buggy was almost brand-new, and Brad obviously spent a lot of time keeping it up.

Brad glanced up, grinned, and waved. "Hi,

kid," he called casually. "Where's that beautiful big sister of yours?"

"She's getting changed," Hilary said, leaning over the railing and feeling resentful. Brad always called her "kid," as if she were twelve years old and wore her hair in pigtails. But he was nineteen, and Hilary thought wearily that to him, she probably *did* seem like a kid.

Brad was wearing his usual outfit: shorts, sandals, and a T-shirt that was cut off above his waist to show off his bronzed stomach muscles. He worked on a charter boat that took fishermen out into the Gulf to catch red snapper and sea trout, and he spent his spare time surfing.

"Amy bought a new dress for the dance, but she didn't want you to see her in it," Hilary said to make conversation.

"Oh, yeah?" Lazily, Brad leaned against the dune buggy, cracking his knuckles. "How come?"

Hilary gave a careless shrug. "How should I know? Maybe Cinderella's afraid she'll turn into a pumpkin. Maybe it's not exactly the right dress for her. Maybe it makes her look skinny or something."

Brad chuckled. "Skinny, huh? Somehow, I don't think so. Amy isn't exactly what you'd call skinny. She's just right, in all the right places." He looked up at Hilary with a playful, exaggerated leer. "Speaking of the right places, kid, I notice that you're, ah, beginning to grow up. Howie keeps asking me when we're going to double-date again. You know, you really impressed the guy. He just can't wait to tell you all about the new computer programs he's written."

Hilary groaned. "Tell Howie he can stuff it," she muttered.

Howie was Brad's cousin, and Amy and Brad had arranged a date for Hilary with him. Howie had turned out to be a computer wizard, who could only talk about the programs he was writing. It had been a terrible evening.

"Well, maybe Howie isn't your type anymore," said Brad. "Maybe I ought to look around for somebody a little older and wiser." He winked. "How about it, little sister? Should I fix you up with one of the big boys?"

Blushing furiously, Hilary stood up straight and crossed her arms over her chest. "I am *not* your little sister," she said between clenched teeth. "And you and Amy can just stop trying to fix me up. I don't need your help."

At that moment Amy came out onto the deck. "Hey, what's going on here?" she asked, turning to Hilary. "Do you have to start fights with everyone?"

"How come you assume that *I'm* the one

who started it?" Hilary demanded, feeling tears close to the surface.

"Listen, Hilary, I'm sorry," Brad called from below. His voice was contrite. "I was just joking. I didn't mean—"

"Yes, you did." Hilary tried to swallow past the hurt in her throat. "You and Amy are always on my case about going out with somebody. And I want you to stop it!"

"We're just trying to help, Hilary." Amy said reasonably. She stepped forward and put her hand on Hilary's shoulder. "I don't know what Brad said, but whatever it was—"

"Leave me alone," Hilary said, backing off. "I don't need anybody's help. Not yours or Brad's or—"

"Girls, girls, stop that quarreling!" Mrs. Malone came to the door, wiping her hands on a towel. "I could hear you all the way in the kitchen. Do you have to argue in front of Brad?"

"Who cares?" Hilary said grimly, stalking past Amy and hoping Brad would hear her. "He's just the latest one in Amy's long list of boyfriends. In a few weeks there'll be somebody else hanging around, acting macho, and trying to impress her. So why should I worry what this one thinks?"

"Hilary!" Mrs. Malone gasped.

"Hey, what's going on up there?" Brad

called. "Listen, Hilary, I'm sorry if I hurt your feelings. I was just fooling around. Really. How about if you go for a ride with Amy and me?" He patted the dune buggy's fender. "There's room for three if we scrunch up a little."

Mrs. Malone turned with a warning look to her older daughter. "Amy, I want you to remember what I told you about riding in Brad's dune buggy," she cautioned. "And that goes for you, too, Hilary."

With a dull sense of satisfaction, Hilary ignored the look of silent entreaty that Amy threw in her direction. "I wouldn't get into that contraption for anything," she said. "It's not safe."

Amy stepped back as if Hilary had slapped her. "You're just saying that because you don't like Brad," she said angrily, speaking softly so that Brad wouldn't hear her. "You're trying to spoil my fun the way you always do, just because you don't have any fun of your own." She turned pleading eyes to her mother. "It's perfectly safe, Mom, really. All the kids ride around in buggies, and nobody ever gets hurt." She took her mother by the arm and pulled her to the railing, pointing down at the dune buggy. "See, it's got a roll bar and seat belts and everything. And Brad's a terrific driver. Nothing's going to happen."

"Hi, Brad," Mrs. Malone said, smiling cheerfully down at him. Then she turned to her daughter and patted her on the arm. "You're absolutely right, Amy. Nothing's going to happen because you're going to find something safer to ride around in." She glanced up at the dark clouds that now hung directly over the house. "Anyway, it's going to rain in a few minutes." Leaning down over the railing, she called to Brad, "Why don't you come up and have supper with us? We're having chowder tonight, and I seem to remember that you like chowder."

"Great! Thanks," Brad said, heading for the stairs.

With a stern look, Mrs. Malone turned to Hilary, who was standing in the doorway. "Hilary, come into the kitchen. I want to talk with you."

The chowder pot was beginning to bubble on the stove, and its rich fragrance filled the air. Mrs. Malone gestured toward a high stool by the counter. "Sit down for a few minutes, Hilary. We need to talk."

Reluctantly Hilary pulled out the stool and climbed onto it, hooking her heels over the rungs. "I know I shouldn't have said that about Brad," she admitted, avoiding her mother's accusing eyes.

"You're right. You shouldn't have said that about Brad," Mrs. Malone replied matter-offactly. "It was inexcusably rude." She placed a bowl of strawberries and a knife in front of Hilary. "Would you please help me slice these?"

Hilary picked up the knife. "I'm sorry," she said sullenly. "I don't know why I did it."

Mrs. Malone sat down across the counter with another knife and a bowl and reached for a strawberry. "It isn't so much what happened this afternoon that troubles me, Hilary. It's what's been happening for the past several months. You and your sister used to get along so well. You hardly ever fought. But now it seems as if the two of you—and I'm not blaming either one of you—go out of your way to be sure there's an argument every day and a major battle once a week."

"Well, then," Hilary protested, putting down her knife, "you should talk to Amy, too. It's not fair to lecture just me."

"I know she's as much at fault," Mrs. Malone said. "And I *have* spoken with her—this afternoon while we were shopping. She's promised to be more careful about your feelings, and I want you to be more careful about hers. Is it a deal?"

For a moment Hilary sat still. Finally she said, "I'll try."

"That's all I ask, honey," Mrs. Malone said softly. She reached out to pat Hilary's hand. "I know it hasn't been easy for you since your father moved to Houston. Maybe that's had something—"

"How can you blame Dad?" Hilary demanded angrily, jerking her hand back. "He's got nothing to do with the way Amy and I act." She slid off the stool and stood up. "I don't want to talk about it anymore. I'm going outside." Before she turned to go, she saw that her mother's eyes were filling with tears, but she didn't turn back.

Chapter Three

Hilary was awakened early the next morning by her mother knocking on the door. "Hilary," she said, "I have to drive over to the mainland on business today, so Elena's going to need some help in the shop. I'd be grateful if you could fill in for me."

Hilary pushed back her covers and sat up. She had spent a restless night, and she felt sluggish and tired. But she had liked working in the shop on the few occasions when Elena or her mother had needed another helper. There was always a new and interesting painting or piece of sculpture to see in the gallery and very interesting people to meet in the shop. The artists on the island—and there was a fairly large group of them—stopped in often, and Hilary enjoyed talking with them about their work. Being with Elena was fun, too, Hilary thought, although she was sometimes a little unsettling. Elena had a way of making you see an issue in a new light, even if you thought you already understood it.

The White Pelican was located in an old fishing camp that had been made over into clusters of small shops and boutiques. The store was really two stores in one—a shop where artists could buy all kinds of painting and craft supplies, and a gallery where the very best were invited to display their work for sale. Hilary's mother, who had a degree in business, managed the shop and helped in the gallery, while Elena managed the gallery and helped in the shop. The two were a good team, and The White Pelican had prospered.

Hilary had ridden her bike to the shop. She put it in the rack and went inside. It was early for tourists, so the gallery was deserted. But there were already six local customers in the shop, which had its own entrance but was connected to the gallery by a large open door.

Standing behind the cash register, Elena flashed a smile of relief at Hilary. She was wearing a loose white shirt with a heavy rope of red beads and a pair of baggy red pants, and her dark hair was pulled up into a loose bun held in place with a giant wooden pin. "Thank heavens you're here," she whispered. "We're swamped already."

For the next hour, Hilary and Elena were busy with customers. Finally things slowed down a little, and Elena glanced at her watch. "It's only eleven o'clock," she said, "but it feels as though we've already done a full day's business. Did you notice the man with the beard? He bought an easel, half a dozen brushes, and nearly fifty dollars worth of paints!"

"And I had a forty-dollar sale," Hilary said, leafing through the sales slips. "It was Mrs. Madison from the day-care center. She was buying brushes and paints for the kids."

"Super! Well, it's time we relaxed a little, wouldn't you say? Let's reward ourselves." Elena disappeared into the office at the back of the gallery and returned with two cans of cold soda. As she handed one to Hilary, she said, "I haven't seen you for a week or so. How's your painting coming along? Do you have any new work to show me?"

Hilary snapped the can open, thinking of the watercolor she had torn up. "I'm afraid not," she said a little reluctantly. "I was working on something, but—"

"But what?"

"Oh, nothing. It just didn't turn out, that's all. Anyway, yesterday I did some pencil

32

sketches that I think are pretty good." Hilary thought briefly about Jason. "Maybe after we close this afternoon I'll go back to the dunes and do a little experimenting."

Elena gave her a measuring look. "And how are you and Amy doing these days?"

Hilary frowned and took a drink. Elena had a way of getting directly to the heart of things. Although Hilary had recently mentioned to Elena that she and Amy had been arguing, she wasn't sure that was why Elena was asking. Hilary wondered if her mother had said something to Elena over the phone that morning. "Did Mom tell you about last night?" she asked suspiciously.

Elena shook her head. "Is there something to tell? You looked a little down when you came in this morning, so I thought something might be going on. Haven't you two straightened everything out yet?"

"No, and I don't think we're going to," Hilary said unhappily. She held the half-empty can to her cheek, enjoying its cool dampness. "Everything seems to turn into a quarrel, no matter what." She sighed. "Sometimes it's her fault, like the time she yelled at me for tracking a bit of sand onto her rug. But sometimes it's my fault—like last night." She shook her head. "It started when I made a tacky remark to Brad about Amy's new dress. I don't really know why I said it, except that he makes me mad when he calls me kid. I'm *not* a kid! Anyway, then Amy got in on it, and she made me so angry that I said something *really* nasty about Brad."

Elena looked at her curiously. "For heaven's sake, what did you say?"

"I said that Brad was just the latest in Amy's long line of boyfriends." Hilary hung her head. "I wanted him to get the idea that he wasn't anybody special."

"You're right. That wasn't a very nice thing to say, although it might be true." Elena tipped up the can and finished her soft drink. "Have you talked with Amy? If the two of you could figure out what's behind all the arguments—"

"Mom thinks that Dad's responsible," Hilary said unhappily. Now that she thought about it, she almost felt worse about what her mother had said than about her argument with Amy. "It really upset me when she said it. I don't think it's fair to blame him. He isn't even here. How could he have anything to do with our fights when he's more than three hundred miles away?"

"I don't think she was blaming your father in *that* sense, Hilary," Elena answered thoughtfully. "I think she just meant that the way you and Amy *feel* about your dad may be making you edgy and irritable, so it's harder for you to behave in a reasonable fashion and get along with each other." She looked concerned. "Having your father move out must have been a pretty tough thing for both of you—but maybe even harder for *you*. Just from watching you and your dad together, I always thought the two of you were awfully good friends."

Hilary nodded, blinking away the tears that suddenly clouded her eyes. "Amy and Mom are so close that sometimes—well, sometimes they make me feel left out because they have such fun together. I think about Dad a lot, and I really feel mixed up. I know I shouldn't care about him since he's the one who left us. . . ." Her voice trailed off.

"There's no rule that says you shouldn't love your dad." Elena put her arm around Hilary. "Whether he's here on the island or in Houston or wherever, he's still your father."

"But he *left* us!" Hilary burst out angrily. "How can you keep on loving a person when he does something like that?"

Elena's arm tightened. "That's a real puzzle, Hilary. But we often love people without knowing why," she said softly. "We love them for *themselves*, not because of what they do or don't do. Love isn't always based on logic, you know."

Hilary nodded slowly. Just then, the brass bells over the door jingled. Hilary looked up and froze. Jason Wolf was coming through the door. In a minute he would see her! She thought of their meeting on the dunes and cringed inside. She had behaved like a stubborn child, and she didn't want to face him. "I—I'll be back in a minute," she muttered and tried to push past Elena to the back of the shop.

But just at that moment a customer walked into the gallery, and Elena turned to go. "Isn't that Jason Wolf?" she asked. "Why don't you take care of him, and I'll get the gallery."

Trapped, Hilary waited nervously for Jason to come to the counter. He was wearing crisp khaki shorts and a white T-shirt with a vivid red paint stain across one sleeve. His dark hair was tousled.

"Hello, Hilary," Jason said. His voice was sober, but there was a smile in his blue eyes. "I didn't know you worked here."

"I don't, really. I'm just helping out for the day," Hilary replied in a low voice. She could feel a flush rising above the collar of her blouse.

Jason didn't seem to notice. "I came in to get some canvas," he said. "Can you cut it for me?"

"Sure." Hilary tried to make her voice

matter-of-fact. "How much do you need?" As she led the way to the rack where the rolls of canvas were kept, she could feel Jason's eyes on her, and goose bumps rose on her arms. She hoped he had forgotten what had happened on the dunes.

"Six yards," he said, close behind her.

"You must be working on a big project," Hilary said as she pulled out the canvas.

"Right. Two big oils, as a matter of fact." He watched her closely, almost as if he were studying her features. "If they turn out, I'll enter both of them in the art festival in August. I was wondering if—" He paused as if he were going to say something else, then added, "Are you entering anything?"

Hilary measured and cut the canvas, working deliberately. She was finding it hard to concentrate with Jason standing so close. She barely knew this boy—why did he make her feel so uncomfortable? "I'm not sure," she said without looking up. "I don't really have anything good enough to enter yet."

"I'll bet that's not true," Jason replied with a teasing grin as they went back to the cash register. "What I've seen of your work is pretty good. Too good to tear up, anyway."

Hilary glanced sideways at Jason. So he hadn't forgotten after all. She sighed. "I guess I ought to apologize to you—about the other

37

evening, I mean. I shouldn't have torn up the watercolor. You were just trying to help, and I sort of overreacted."

"So I noticed," Jason said with a cheerful grin, and Hilary noticed how white and even his teeth were. "But don't worry about it. It happens to everybody once in a while. I'm just sorry about the watercolor. You had a good thing going there."

Hilary turned away. "The canvas is three dollars a yard," she said in a businesslike tone. "That'll be eighteen dollars, plus ninety cents tax." As she counted out his change, their fingers touched, and Hilary pulled her hand back as if she had been burned. Flustered, she looked up, and her eyes met Jason's. "Thank—thank you," she said. "Please come back." The minute she said it, she wished she hadn't. Would he think she was giving him a personal invitation? No, of course not. It was just an automatic thing to say, like writing "Miss you" at the end of a letter when you really didn't mean it.

"I'll do that," Jason said, his eyes still on hers. "Especially if you're going to be here." Without another word, he put his change in his pocket and left the store, the roll of canvas tucked under his arm.

Hilary stared after him. Jason Wolf wanted to see *her*? That was ridiculous! He was going with Cindy—and even if he weren't, he could have his pick of all the girls. Why would he bother with her? What in the world could he have meant?

Chapter Four

It was getting dark when Hilary came back from the dunes where she had been working on her watercolors after work. Mrs. Malone was in the front room, reading the Port Isabel paper. "Amy and I just had sandwiches for supper," she said. "I made an extra one for you. It's in the refrigerator, and there's a pitcher of iced tea, too. Help yourself."

"Thanks, Mom." Impulsively Hilary went over to her mother and hugged her.

"Mmm, nice," Mrs. Malone murmured appreciatively. "What did I do to deserve that?"

"Oh, nothing special," Hilary replied, a little embarrassed. "You're just a pretty neat mother, that's all." She hesitated. "Look, I'm sorry about last night. About what happened in the kitchen, I mean. I know you didn't mean to criticize Dad. And maybe you're right—partly, anyway. It's something I have to think about some more."

"I wish you would," Mrs. Malone said. There was a troubled look in her eyes. "Something else has come up, Hilary. Amy has something important to tell you." She paused, and her voice was serious. "No matter how *you* feel about what she says, honey, try to understand how *she's* feeling. Things may not work out the way she wants them to, but now isn't the time to tell her that."

"OK," Hilary said, puzzled by her mother's words. "But I'm going to get my sandwich first. Painting gives me an appetite—especially when it goes well."

It *had* gone very well. Working from the sketches she had done the day before, Hilary experimented with a looser style, brushing on the paint more quickly than ever before. The work that she'd done that day, she decided as she got the sandwich out of the refrigerator, was better than anything she had done for a long time.

"Mom said you had something to tell me," Hilary said a few minutes later, putting her head into Amy's room. "Can I eat my sandwich in here?"

"Sure." Amy was sitting in front of her dressing table, brushing her hair, which fanned out over her shoulders in a golden cascade. "Just be careful of the crumbs, that's all." She turned around as Hilary took off her shoes and sat on the bed. "I've got some news for you."

"That's what Mom said," Hilary replied, taking a sip of her iced tea. Sometimes Amy liked to dramatize things, and it took a little while to get to the point. "So, tell me your news. What's all the mystery?"

A frown crossed Amy's face as if she didn't like being rushed. "There's no mystery," she said. "I just wanted to tell you that Brad and I have made a pretty big decision. We've decided to get married. Oh, not right away," she added hastily. "Brad's going to buy me an engagement ring in a few months, just as soon as he gets his dune buggy paid for, and we're going to get married sometime next winter, when we've got enough money to get an apartment over in Port Isabel."

Hilary swallowed a bite of her sandwich, but it stuck in her throat, which seemed suddenly dry. It was true she had looked forward to the day when Amy would go away to college. And she'd been disappointed when her sister had decided to stay at home and go to school nearby. But Amy leaving to *get married*? That was different. It seemed like such a permanent thing! "Are you sure you're ready to be engaged?" she asked doubtfully.

Amy's face started to cloud, and Hilary hurried on. "I mean, you have another whole year of junior college, and then I thought you were going to go on and finish your degree. Won't you have to work full-time to have an apartment? Working and going to college might be pretty tough." She tried to picture Brad as Amy's husband but failed. She kept seeing him on his surfboard, and the idea seemed incongruous. She shook her head. "What's Brad going to do? Keep his job on the fishing boat? Where will he work while you're in college?"

Amy bristled. "Is there anything wrong with working on a fishing boat?" she asked icily. "It's a perfectly respectable job, even though it doesn't bring in a lot of money. And I really don't know if I want to go to college right now. Maybe later." She looked as if she were going to cry. "Hilary, I'm getting *engaged*, for heaven's sake. Aren't you even a little bit happy for me?"

"Of course, I'm happy for you," Hilary said contritely. She sat on the edge of the bed and tried to smile. "It's just that a few months is a long time, and you and Brad might change your minds by then."

Amy slammed the hairbrush onto her dressing table. "Oh, Hilary, you're absolutely impossible!" she burst out angrily. "I might have known you'd find a way to try and spoil my happiness! You always do!"

"I'm not trying to spoil anything," Hilary said as reasonably as she could. "Brad is a nice guy, but so are some of the other guys you've dated. And you have to admit that you've been in love a couple of times before Brad came along. I just think you ought to wait a little before you get engaged, that's all."

"How could I have expected you to understand?" Amy said. Her voice was heavy with sarcasm and her mouth twisted. "You don't know how it feels. You've never been in love. In fact, no boy has ever paid the slightest bit of attention to you!"

"That's all you know," Hilary muttered, remembering what Jason had said. "Just today—" She stopped, thinking she had gone too far, and plucked at the lace on Amy's pink bedspread.

"Well, who is it?" Amy asked mockingly. "What tall, handsome prince has asked poor little Cinderella for a date?"

"It wasn't like that," Hilary said defensively, feeling the familiar resentment well up inside her. Why did Amy always make her feel this way? "And if you have to know, it was Jason Wolf."

"Jason Wolf?" Amy hooted. "Who are you trying to kid, Hilary? Jason Wolf has been going with Cindy Morris for the last two years. The Jason and Cindy show is the longest running act at Port Isabel High School. He's not even available! And if he were, he'd be going out with somebody *really* cute and popular." She didn't add "not with somebody like you," but the words hung between them just as if she had said them.

Hilary flinched. Of course, Amy was right. Jason couldn't be interested in her. "I didn't say we were going out together," she said desperately. "I just said—"

"And *I* just said Brad and I were going to get engaged, and you had to throw cold water on it." Amy's voice was rising dangerously, and there was a sob in it. "You never want me to be happy. Just because *you're* miserable all the time, you want to spoil things for everybody else!"

"That's not true!" Hilary shouted, jumping up from the bed. "You're just getting on my case so you won't have to think about what I said about changing your mind! Because it's true and you know it! People change their minds!" Tears spilled down her cheeks, and she wiped them away angrily.

"Girls, what in the world is going on here?" Mrs. Malone stood in the door, looking from one daughter to the other in dismay. "Both of you promised you'd put a stop to this awful fighting!"

Amy ran to her bed and flung herself across it, crying. "I just wanted her to say that she was happy about Brad and me," she said, sobbing. "And all she could say was that we'd probably change our minds! She doesn't want me to be happy—with Brad or anybody else!"

Trembling, Hilary looked at her sister. "What I said is true," she said, her throat tight with pain. "People change their minds. Dad changed his mind, didn't he? He decided he didn't want to live with us anymore. So maybe Brad will change his mind—or maybe you will, for that matter, Amy."

"All that may be true," Mrs. Malone said sadly, holding out her hand to Hilary. "But tonight isn't the night to say it. Tonight is a time to think happy thoughts about two people who care enough about each other to plan on spending their lives together." She glanced at Amy with the same troubled look that Hilary had seen earlier. "Maybe they'll change their minds as they think about everything that's involved. Or maybe something will happen to change their plans. But tonight your sister wants you to be as happy as she is about her decision. That's not too much to ask, is it?"

Hilary realized her mom was right. Amy only wanted to hear good things; she didn't want to be realistic. Hilary took a deep breath. "Well, then, Amy, all I can say is that I wish you all the happiness in the world. I hope you and Brad stay happy together, just the way you are tonight." There. She'd said it. But the words sounded stiff and mechanical, and Hilary knew they wouldn't satisfy Amy.

Amy sat up; her eyes were red, and her face was tear streaked. "Did you hear that?" she cried furiously, pounding the bed with her fist. "She doesn't mean a word of it, Mom. She's just saying it because she has to!"

"Now, Amy, I think it's time you settled down," Mrs. Malone said firmly. She went over to the bed and pushed the damp hair off Amy's forehead. "Hilary, why don't you leave Amy and me to talk for a while."

"Yeah, sure," Hilary said, going to the door. It was always the same. She was left out, always an extra, while her mother and Amy were a pair. "Sure," she repeated dully and left the room.

The early-morning sun had risen well above the horizon when Hilary started up the beach the next day. She was wearing a blue swim-

47

suit under a pair of faded cut-offs. Her lunch was tucked into her day pack, along with her watercolor box and folding easel. She decided to hike to Shell Beach, four miles up the seashore to the north, and spend the morning doing quick watercolor studies of shells and driftwood.

The warm Gulf currents swept all kinds of fascinating treasures ashore on Shell Beach. One could find dozens of varieties of shells— fluted scallops and cockles, elegant angel wings and sand dollars, and colorful conch shells. One could also pick up intriguing chunks of mahogany, cedar, and balsa, sometimes scoured clean and polished to a shine by the white Gulf sands, sometimes crusted with barnacles and soaked with sea salts, which made the wood burn with eerie green and blue flames in the fireplace.

Ahead of her along the flat beach, a trio of brown sandpipers darted swiftly in and out of the foamy white surf. One sea gull alighted in the shallows to gulp down the small fish he'd caught, while another circled overhead, calling shrilly. An iridescent jellyfish glistened in the sand at the edge of the water, and Hilary avoided it, remembering how her foot had swelled the time she had been stung by one of the creatures. The ocean was green and calm that day, and the sight of the low, slow swells made her feel more peaceful. No matter how stormy her life might be, the ocean and the beach and the dunes always calmed her. That day was no exception, and after a while she was almost able to forget the latest confrontation with Amy.

When Hilary reached Shell Beach, she picked a spot where a long, narrow drift of shells had been carried ashore and put up her easel. Then she selected some of the prettiest shells for her studies and arranged them against a weathered cypress log. She worked for an hour or so while the sun climbed higher in the sky. When she stopped, she had six watercolor studies drying in the sun. These were worth showing to Elena, she thought.

She stripped down to her bathing suit. It was getting warm now—time for a quick dip, and then she'd eat the sandwiches she had brought along.

"Mind if I join you?"

With a start, Hilary turned around. It was Jason. He was wearing white swim trunks and a white T-shirt, and he had on a pair of reflector sunglasses that hid his eyes. In one hand he had a bag of shells, in the other, a camera.

Seeing Jason made Hilary's pulse beat faster. "Are you making a career of sneaking up on people?" she asked uneasily. "How long have you been watching?"

"Long enough to like what I've seen," Jason said with an appreciative grin. "You know, you'd make a very pretty portrait." He slung his camera strap over the easel, then took off his glasses and also put them on the easel. After putting down his shells, he pulled off his T-shirt. "Looks as if you're all ready for a swim. Come on—race you to the water."

For the first few minutes they were in the water together, Hilary was terribly self-conscious. But Jason's easy laughter and his teasing grin soon relaxed her, and to her surprise and pleasure, she began to enjoy herself. They spent the next hour splashing in the surf, swimming just inside the breakers, and building a moated castle at the water's edge.

Finally they shared Hilary's sandwiches and stretched out on the warm sand to dry off. Hilary lay on her stomach, eyes shut and cheek pillowed on her arm, and thought wonderingly about what was happening. Jason lay beside her, his sunglasses reflecting the scene around them like a dark mirror. After ten or fifteen minutes of companionable silence, he turned on his side, facing Hilary, and propped himself up on one elbow. "I followed you up here today," he said. "Partway, anyway. I spotted you walking while I was taking pictures and decided to follow you."

Hilary opened her eyes. His face was very close to hers, but his sunglasses masked his eyes. "Why?" she asked, confused. "Why did you follow me?"

"Because I wanted to see you again. Because I wanted to say I was sorry about the other night." He hesitated. "I shouldn't have been so pushy. You had every right to be angry at me."

"No. I didn't," Hilary said. She rolled over on her back and shading her eyes with her hand, looked at him. "There are a lot of things bothering me these days, and I just sort of took it all out on you. You were only trying to help." She glanced toward the half-dozen watercolors lined up against the log. "And you *did* help, too. The work I did this morning is a lot better because I worked faster without trying to get in too much detail. Your suggestion made a big difference."

Jason pulled off his sunglasses and put his hand on her arm. "Then we're *both* forgiven, right?" He smiled, and the look in his eyes made Hilary tremble. "Friends?"

Hilary's arm seemed to burn where Jason's fingers touched her. "Friends," she whispered. "Except—except—"

Jason sat up. "Except what?" He smiled

51

teasingly. "Are you in the habit of putting conditions on your friendships?"

"Well, no, not exactly," Hilary replied, sitting up after Jason had. She had a tricky question to ask Jason, and it made her feel awkward. If she were Amy, she'd come up with some clever way to ask the question. But she wasn't, and she couldn't think of any way to ask it except straight out. "You're going with Cindy Morris," she said quietly. "Doesn't that sort of put conditions on a friendship with another girl?"

Jason looked at her, but Hilary couldn't read his eyes. "I guess you haven't heard," he said flatly. "Cindy's dad got transferred to Chicago just before school let out. They've already moved."

"Oh, Jason, I'm sorry," Hilary said, trying to disguise the relief that crept into her voice. "It—it must have been hard to say goodbye."

Jason picked up a small pink shell and examined it carefully. "No, it wasn't, really," he said. "In fact, I'd been thinking that maybe it wasn't a very good idea to keep on going with her." He turned the shell over in his fingers. "People change. It was time for Cindy and me to stop being so exclusive." He glanced at Hilary. "But I have to admit that it would have been hard for me to tell her so. When she told me she was moving, that sort of took care of the problem."

Hilary stared out at the green ocean, thinking over Jason's words: "People change." So she wasn't the only one who had learned that lesson. "I'm sorry about you and Cindy," she said quietly. "But you're right about people changing." She thought about her father. "You can't really depend on anyone but yourself," she added, and there was a bitter edge to her voice.

Jason dropped the shell and took her hand. "That's not what I meant at all, Hilary. You've *got* to depend on other people—that's part of being human. But you can't *trap* people by depending on them. We all need room to grow. It was a good thing for Cindy and me to change, not a *bad* thing." He stood up and brushed the sand off his trunks. "Enough of this heavy stuff. Come on, let's pack up your painting gear. I've got something to show you."

They walked single file for almost a mile back up into the dunes. They didn't talk, and Hilary was glad. There was too much going on inside her head, and she wasn't sure she could trust herself to speak. Jason and Cindy weren't going steady anymore; he had followed her up the beach; he'd said he wanted to be friends. What did he mean? Could he possibly mean—? Hilary shook her head in disbelief. No, he just meant *friends*, that was all. But she could still feel the warmth and strength of his fingers around hers, and her heart beat faster as she followed him through the dunes.

Chapter Five

"We're here," Jason announced as they came to the top of a sandy ridge.

Hilary climbed up to stand beside him. "You mean that old boat?" She stared down at a land-locked, derelict wooden tug with a square cabin perched on top, moored to what looked like a pier built in the sand. A long time ago the boat had probably been blue, and Hilary could just make out the words *Princess Pat* painted across the bow in faded red letters. But the curtains at the cabin windows were a bright red, and buckets of red geraniums stood on the deck. In spite of the boat's run-down look, there was something jaunty and cheerful about it.

"This is Sam's place," Jason said. "The *Princess Pat*." He grinned at Hilary. "Most people

55

think Sam's a little crazy, but I think you'll like him. Especially when you see what he does for a hobby. He's someone special." With Jason leading the way, Hilary clambered down the dune. When they reached the pier, she saw that there was a rope ladder hanging over the side. Obviously, Sam's visitors had to be skilled rope-climbers.

Jason cupped his hands around his mouth. "Hey, Sam, you home?" he called.

Somewhere a dog began to bark wildly, and in a minute a man wearing a captain's hat appeared over the rail above them. "Well, hello, Jason," the man drawled, smiling widely. "Come on aboard, and bring your friend."

"Go on, it's safe," Jason said as Hilary looked dubiously at the rope ladder. "I'm right behind you."

In a minute they stood on deck. It had obviously been freshly scrubbed because there were still puddles of water on it, and a mop was leaning against the deck railing.

"Hilary, this is Sam," Jason said. "Samuel James, captain and super wood-carver."

"It's nice to meet you, Sam," Hilary said shyly, holding out her hand. Sam was short and stooped, with an untidy gray beard that grew down over his wrinkled brown throat. But his pale blue eyes twinkled, and his smile was almost mischievous. He wore an old blue work shirt with the sleeves rolled up, and his captain's hat sat at a rakish angle on his head.

"Glad you could come, glad you could come," Sam said, beaming proudly. "And Merriweather's glad, too, from the looks of her." Merriweather, a small, brown dog with a red bandanna around her neck, was sniffling noisily at Hilary's feet. "Now, Merriweather, don't be such a nuisance," Sam cautioned. Gently, he pushed the dog away with his foot. "Why don't you folks come down below and have some lemonade."

"We were at Shell Beach today, and I wanted Hilary to see your carvings," Jason said as Sam led the way down a rickety wooden ladder and into the cool darkness below the deck. "Not to mention *Princess Pat.*"

"Good old Patsy," Sam said tenderly as they walked along a narrow passageway. "We've been together for a long while now, good times and bad." He turned and grinned at Hilary. "The Lady Pat and I sailed together out of Brownsville years ago, when both of us were young and spry and ornery. When we got too old to try to second-guess the Gulf any longer, we decided it was time to retire. Took a *big* truck to haul the old girl out here, but this is where she belongs—high and dry, but in sight and sound of the ocean." He patted the bulk-head. "Let's see—lemonade, wasn't it?"

The boat seemed to be divided across its width into three small rooms, with the galley in the middle and Sam's sleeping quarters in the stern. There wasn't room in the tiny galley for all three of them, so Hilary went on down the narrow passageway toward the bow and into the living room—or what would have been called a living room in an ordinary house. It was a long, narrow room with a row of round, evenly spaced portholes cut in one side and a skylight in the deck above, flooding the scrubbed wooden floor with light. Sam obviously used the room as his workshop, for there was a workbench piled with tools and scraps of wood and several half-finished pieces. Hilary picked one up and examined it curiously. It was a carving of a wood duck, its head and neck lovingly shaped into a graceful curve.

"Here's what they look like when Sam's fin-ished with them," Jason said, coming up behind her. He pointed to a long shelf that ran the length of the room, crowded with carved gulls, ducks, and herons. Some of the birds were caught in the act of fishing, some were poised for flight, and some were soaring grace-fully, wings spread wide. "Most of these are carved from driftwood that Sam picked up on beaches all around the Gulf," he continued. "But he concentrates on Shell Beach. He says more interesting pieces of driftwood wash up there than anywhere else."

Hilary stared at the crowded shelf. "Jason, they're amazing!" she whispered wonderingly. She touched a tall heron that stood gracefully on one slender leg as if it were ready to dip into the water for a fish. "I've never seen carvings so beautiful! Sam's a real artist!"

"Why now, thank you, young lady," Sam said in a pleased voice, coming from the galley with a frosty pitcher of lemonade and three glasses. He pulled out a small table and pointed to a pile of cushions on the floor. "Make yourselves comfortable."

Hilary sat down cross-legged on a purple cushion, next to Jason. "How long have you been carving?" she asked eagerly. "Have you exhibited your sculptures in any art shows?"

Sam threw back his head and laughed. "Hear that, Merriweather?" he asked in a stage whisper, bending over so that he could talk into Merriweather's ear. "She wants to know if I've exhibited any of my whittlings. What do you think of that?" Merriweather cocked her head and gave a short, amused bark. "My sentiments exactly," Sam said. He straightened up. "Why, bless you, Miss Hilary, those ain't sculptures. They ain't carvings, either. They're just whittlings, that's all."

Hilary started to interrupt, but Sam went on. "And I'm no artist, though you're sure kind to say so. I'm just an old man with nimble fingers, an eye for detail, and a good sharp pocketknife." He poured three glasses of lemonade and handed one to Jason and another to Hilary. "I've been whittling for fifty years, on and off, like my pa and my grandpa before me. But it's just a hobby, just a way to pass the time and keep these old fingers from getting stiff." He nodded wisely. "Artists are folks with *real* talent. Like Jason here. You ever seen this young man's painting? Why, he's the very best, he is. He's got *real* talent." He put a hand on Jason's shoulder. "*Real* talent."

"I've been trying to convince Sam that he should enter some of his carvings in the art festival," Jason said, turning to Hilary. "Maybe you can talk him into it."

Sam shook his head emphatically. "No, sir, ain't no way I'm going to show off this stuff. It ain't art. Why, everybody would laugh when they saw me driving up with a load of whittlings."

"Sam, that's just not true," Hilary said earnestly. "No one would *dare* to laugh. Why, your carvings are better than any I've ever seen at the festival—or in any of the shops on the mainland, for that matter. And I ought to know what I'm talking about. My mom is a partner in The White Pelican, an art gallery in the village, and sometimes I work there. I see what's on display every week. They've never had a piece of wood sculpture as fine as the carvings you've got here."

Sam hunched his shoulders and began to scowl as if he were about to say something. Jason threw a quick warning look at Hilary. "Sam," he said, breaking in, "forget about the festival. Why don't you tell Hilary about the time you and *Princess Pat* rode out the big hurricane?"

Sam's scowl disappeared as if by magic, and for the next hour he entertained them with stories of his exploits in his tug.

When they got ready to leave, Sam stood up and bowed to Hilary. "I thank you for your company, Miss Hilary," he said in a formal tone. "I don't often get to tell my stories to somebody who's never heard them before."

Hilary took the hand he held out. His fingers were bent and crooked, but his grasp was firm. "Can we come back sometime?" she asked. Then she flushed. It sounded as if she were inviting herself—and maybe trying to get Jason to come with her. But Jason just smiled, and Sam looked pleased.

"You truly can. Anytime you want." As

Hilary and Jason climbed to the top of the dune, they could see him standing on the deck, still waving.

"You were right—he's really special," Hilary said as they walked along the beach together, back to the village. "I've never met anybody quite like him."

"He's got a special talent, too," Jason said, splashing through a tide pool. He was barefoot, and his sneakers were knotted together and slung over his shoulder with his camera and shell bag. "I just wish I could get him to enter his work in the festival so that people could see his stuff. He lives out here on practically nothing, but if he could sell some of those carvings for what they're really worth, he could fix up *Princess Pat* and live a lot more comfortably."

They walked a long way without saying anything more, their strides matching easily. Hilary was very much aware of Jason being beside her. But now, after the time they had spent together on the beach and at Sam's, she didn't feel at all uneasy. Instead, she felt relaxed and comfortable, as if she had known Jason for a very long time. But she still felt a tremendous tug of excitement when she looked at him, so tall and strong beside her, and the pounding of her pulse and the shortness of her breath had nothing to do with the fact that they were walking fast.

"There's the trail to my house," Jason said finally, pointing to a narrow path that led over the dune about a half mile from the village. "I promised my mother I'd go over to Port Isabel with her this afternoon, or I'd walk you the rest of the way home. I hope you don't mind."

"No, not at all," Hilary said breathlessly, but she felt a quick pang of regret. She wished he could have walked home with her. *That* would show Amy!

Jason reached for her hand and smiled down at her, but his blue eyes were serious. "It's been a terrific day, Hilary. I want to see you again—soon. Would you like to walk into the village some night and get a pizza or ice cream or something?"

"I'd like that very much," Hilary said in a low voice. And then, before she knew what was happening, Jason bent forward and kissed her on the tip of her nose.

"Thanks for a great day," he said and grinned. Wordlessly, Hilary watched as he turned and walked away.

When Hilary got home, Amy was sitting in a lounge chair on the deck, her hair rolled up on hot rollers, painting her toenails. Hilary frowned. Her skin still tingled from Jason's kiss, and all she wanted to do was to go to her room and shut the door and think about the whole day, detail by detail. She felt as if she were walking, no *floating*, along in a dream, a marvelously exciting, deliriously happy dream, and she didn't want it to come to an end, ever. And she *certainly* didn't want to spoil it by talking with Amy.

But Amy clearly wanted to talk. "About last night," she said abruptly, "I'm sorry, Hilary. I don't know what happened. I guess things just got—out of control."

Hilary stopped reluctantly and shrugged out of her pack, still thinking of Jason. "I'm sorry, too, Amy," she said, turning to go into the house. "I'll really try hard not to let it happen again."

"Don't you think we ought to talk about it?" Amy asked, with an edge of impatience in her voice. She finished painting the nails on one foot and held it out, examining her work critically. "Or are you in a great big hurry to go somewhere?"

Hilary sighed and sat down on the foot of Amy's lounge chair. "No, no hurry," she said. But her happy dream was rapidly disintegrating, and the annoyance she felt came through in her voice. "I just wanted to be by myself for a little while, that's all. Is there anything wrong with that?"

"No, of course not. If you want to be alone, go right ahead. I won't try to stop you. But Mom said you and I ought to talk." Amy pulled the other foot up and began to paint her big toe. "And after what happened last night, I suppose she's right."

Hilary let go of the last tingling recollection of Jason's kiss. "Elena said the same thing," she admitted. "She said there's probably something bothering both of us, and if we could talk out the problem together, maybe we could solve it."

Amy looked crossly at Hilary. "Why did you have to go and talk to Elena?" she demanded. "She's not one of the family. And I don't think it's right for you to talk about me in public."

"She's just as much family as Brad is, maybe even more, and you've probably complained about me to *him*," Hilary protested. "Elena's known both of us for a lot longer than Brad has."

"Well, maybe so, but Brad's going to be part of the family before very long, whether *you* like it or not, Hilary. So you'd better get used to it." There was a long, uncomfortable silence, and then Amy asked, "Well, have you come up with any ideas about what to do?"

"Not really." Hilary sighed wearily. This wasn't going well at all. "It just seems as if we can't have a conversation without getting into a fuss. Like right now."

"But we're not getting into a fuss. We're just discussing."

"Maybe so. But if we're just discussing, why do I feel all edgy and ready to fight? Most of the time when we're talking I feel as if we're competing for something." Hilary was amazed. She hadn't known she felt that way until she heard herself saying it out loud.

Amy put the cap back on the nail polish bottle. "Well, I'm sorry you feel that way, but it's certainly not because of *me*. I can't imagine what we'd be competing for." She undid one roller and tested the curl, glancing at herself in the mirror of her roller set.

"Well, maybe in a way we are," Hilary said thoughtfully. She had come this far; she might just as well go the rest of the way. "Maybe what we're competing for is Mom's attention. You know, you and Mom are such good friends. It always seems as though there's no room for *me*, especially now that Dad's gone. A lot of the time I feel left out. Sort of like an extra thumb or something."

Amy looked up from the mirror. "Hilary, that's just plain ridiculous!" she exclaimed. "Mom and I just happen to enjoy doing the same things, that's all. Nobody's trying to keep you out of anything." She turned back to her mirror and began to pull the other curlers out of her hair. "Anyway, it really bothers me that all you do is wander around on the beach with your paints and your easel. You make it pretty clear that you don't want anybody else around."

Hilary smiled to herself, thinking about Jason. "No, that's not true," she said quietly, watching Amy brush out her shiny, blond curls. "I like having company, when it's somebody who's interested in what I'm doing."

Amy went on as if she hadn't heard. "But that doesn't bother me as much as your know-it-all attitude," she said. "Take last night, for example. Maybe you just wanted to help, like Mom said. But you sounded so *preachy*, like you thought you had all the answers."

Hilary shook her head emphatically. "Well, I don't. But I still think you're awfully young to be engaged. And I certainly think that you and Brad ought to wait for a long time before you go jumping into marriage. It just makes good sense."

"Who cares about making sense when you're in love," Amy said airily. She fluffed up her hair with both hands. "If *you'd* ever been in love, you'd understand. When you're in love, everything's different—exciting." She turned her head, listening to a distant sound.

Hilary heard it, too. It was the roar of Brad's dune buggy turning off the main road. "Just because you're in love, you think that makes anything you want to do perfectly all right," she said. "But it doesn't."

"There you go again." Amy heaved an elaborate sigh and stood up. "Telling me what to do."

"I am *not* telling you what to do," Hilary objected. A feeling of hopelessness filled her. No matter how much they talked, they would never understand each other, she thought. Amy wasn't even listening to what she was saying, but she went on anyway. "I'm just telling you how I *feel* about what you're doing," she said. "There's a difference."

Hilary glanced over the deck railing. Brad's yellow dune buggy was pulled up below, and Brad was standing on the seat. He cupped his hands. "Hey, Amy," he called. "How about going for a ride?"

Amy leaned over the rail. "Well, I don't know," she said hesitantly. "Mom will be home from work in an hour, and if she found out she'd have a fit."

"Aw, come on. Just this once," Brad said coaxingly. "We'll just ride up the beach a little way. We'll be back long before your mom gets home." He winked broadly at Hilary. "Little sister won't tell—will you, kid?"

"Mom *really* doesn't want you to ride in Brad's dune buggy, Amy," Hilary said in a low, urgent voice, trying to keep Brad from hearing. "I don't think you ought to go."

Amy turned away from the railing and scowled. "There you go again, preaching and telling me what to do. I wish you wouldn't meddle in my business, Hilary Malone!"

"I am *not* meddling!" Hilary objected, her voice getting louder and more strained. "I'm just reminding you of how Mom feels."

Amy shot her a defiant look. "And just what gives you the right to tell me how Mom feels?" she asked in a lofty tone. "After all, you're the one who keeps saying that Mom is closer to *me* than to you." She smiled sweetly, but there was a cutting edge to her voice. "And, of course you're right, you know. I'm the one who looks like her, thinks like her. Everyone always says that you're the odd one in the family, remember? You're the one who takes after *Dad*."

There was a peculiar emphasis on the last word, and it grated on Hilary's ears. Suddenly something inside her snapped, and she felt a searing flash of hatred for her sister. For a long moment she couldn't speak, while the hatred burned in her. But when the words finally came out, she was amazed at the icy control that she heard in them. "Well, then, go on and ride with Brad if that's what you want to do." She raised a clenched fist. "I'm not going to stop you. But when you get in trouble, don't ask me to bail you out." Her voice began to tremble, and she took a deep breath, steadying it again. "I don't *care* what happens to you, do you hear me? You could *die,* and I wouldn't care!"

There was a long, churning silence while the two of them stared at each other, and then Amy leaned over the rail again. "I'll just be a minute, Brad," she called sweetly. "I want to get my scarf." She turned back to Hilary, eyes flashing. "I wasn't going to go. But now I will, just to show you that you can't order me around, Miss Know-It-All." She paused deliberately. "Of course, you won't tell Mother where I've gone. That is, unless you're a tattle-tale, too."

Amy left shortly after that, but her taunting words hung in the air. Hilary stood on the deck looking after the dune buggy, tears running down her cheeks. Jason had made it such a perfect day, one of the very best in her whole life. A day of discovery, a day of tender new sensations that made her feel as if she were on the brink of something more beautiful than she had ever imagined. But Amy had ruined all that. And now, whenever she thought of that day, she would think of the bitter, searing hatred she had felt toward her sister and of the way Amy had spoiled those beautiful feelings. It was one more reason to hate her sister.

"Where's Amy?" Mrs. Malone asked when she came home from work an hour later.

"Out with Brad," Hilary said shortly. Amy's taunt still rang in her ears, and she decided not to tell her mother that her sister had gone riding in the dune buggy—unless she was asked directly. Anyway, she couldn't really trust herself to talk about Amy. The hatred still burned inside her, like a pile of glowing coals that refused to be put out. If she said anything at all, her mother would be sure to hear the bitterness in her voice.

"Well, then, let's you and I have some supper together," Mrs. Malone said briskly, going into the kitchen. "Amy can have leftovers when she gets home. How about giving me a hand?"

Hilary followed her mother into the kitchen. Mrs. Malone opened the refrigerator and began to get out salad makings. "How was your day, honey?" she asked.

Hilary thought, *Until the argument with Amy, it was a marvelous day.* "Terrific," she said, forcing Amy from her thoughts and concentrating on Jason. He had followed her to Shell Beach on purpose. He had taken her to meet his friend Sam. And he had kissed her! If she tried hard, she could focus on all those beautiful things, and not on the ugliness of her feelings about Amy. "It was terrific," she said again, and this time it sounded as if she meant it.

"Well, that's nice," her mother said absently, rinsing off a head of broccoli. "What did you do?"

Hilary got out some silverware and set the kitchen table. "I took my watercolor box and easel up to Shell Beach and did about six watercolors. Then Jason Wolf came along, and we went swimming. Then we went to see a friend of his, who's a wood-carver and lives in an old boat up in the dunes. And then we walked home together. That's all." *Well, almost all,* she thought.

Mrs. Malone glanced curiously at her daughter and handed her a tomato and a knife. "Here, slice this, please. We'll have it with some fresh dill and yogurt and some raw broccoli." She paused. "Jason Wolf? Isn't he the boy who won first prize at the state art fair last year with his oils?"

Hilary nodded and cut a thick slice from the tomato. "Yes, that's Jason. He and his family moved over here from the mainland after school was out." Not looking up, she added,

"He was going steady with Cindy Morris, but she moved away."

"Oh." Mrs. Malone regarded her daughter thoughtfully. "Do I detect a new interest here?"

Hilary smiled. It was so nice to be talking to her mother like this. "I think so," she said, blushing a little. "He asked me if we could go out one night, and I said—"

Just then the phone rang. "Excuse me," Mrs. Malone said, holding up her hand. "Let's go on with this in a minute. I want to hear more about Jason." While her mother went to answer the phone, Hilary looked in the cupboard for a plate for the sliced tomato. She was only half-listening, but when she heard her mother moan, "Oh, no!" she turned quickly.

Mrs. Malone was clutching the receiver, her face ashen. "How is she?" she asked in a low voice. There was a brief silence while Mrs. Malone listened to the voice on the other end.

"Mom, what's happened?" Hilary cried.

"I see. I'll be there as soon as I can."

"Mother! What's happened?" Hilary repeated frantically. "What's going on?"

"It's Amy," Mrs. Malone said. She hung up the phone and leaned weakly against the wall, her face starting to crumple. "She's been in an accident. She was out with Brad in that awful dune buggy of his. They're both in the hospital in Port Isabel! Oh, Hilary, she's very badly hurt!"

Chapter Six

Hilary was hunched up miserably in the corner of the uncomfortable leather sofa in the hospital waiting room, where she had been sitting with her mother and Elena for the last four hours, scarcely talking. It was nearly ten o'clock, and the sounds of the hospital had quieted around them. All she could think about was Amy lying white and frighteningly still in the operating room down the hall.

Hilary looked down at her hands clenched in her lap, and her eyes blurred with tears. The accident was *her* fault, she thought. She could hear the angry echoes of her own voice ringing in her ears. *I don't care what happens to you. You could die, and I wouldn't care!* But that wasn't true. She hadn't meant it. And Amy had known that—hadn't she? *You could die . . . you could die . . . you could die.* Had she meant it? Had she hated her sister so much at that moment that she really *wanted* her to die? Hilary hugged herself and rocked back and forth miserably. Her stomach muscles were tightly knotted, and she could hardly breathe. She felt like crying, and though the tears were there, deep inside her, they wouldn't come.

At that moment her mother stood up from her chair and took a couple of steps forward. "Mike!" she exclaimed. "Oh, Mike, I'm so glad you're here!"

Hilary looked up, her mouth suddenly parched. Her father was standing in the doorway. His tie was loosened and his reddish-brown hair, so like her own, was completely mussed up, as if he'd been running his fingers through it.

"I came as soon as I got your message," he said hoarsely, his face drawn and white. "I was lucky—I got the last seat on the eight o'clock plane to Brownsville and picked up a rented car there." He looked at Hilary's mother. "How is she, Meg?" Then, as Mrs. Malone began to cry, he crossed the room in two strides and put his arms around her protectively. "She's going to be all right, isn't she?" he murmured, his mouth against her hair, his eyes closed. His arms tightened around her. "Isn't she?"

Mrs. Malone's shoulders began to shake, and she didn't answer. Hilary tried to speak, but her voice wouldn't work, and she felt as if she were frozen. Finally Elena spoke from the other side of the room.

"They don't know yet, Mike," she said quietly. "Or if they know, they haven't told us. They just said that she has very serious back injuries and that there appears to be some paralysis." She looked at her watch. "The doctor said he'd talk to us in a few minutes."

Mr. Malone took a deep breath and dropped his arms. "What happened?" His voice was taut and strained.

Again it was Elena who answered. "Amy was out riding with Brad in his dune buggy, and somebody pulled out in front of them. They weren't going very fast, but there was loose gravel on the road, and Brad apparently lost control. The police say his dune buggy rolled over a couple of times. Amy wasn't wearing a seat belt, and she was thrown out onto the sand."

"A dune buggy? Oh, my God. And was Brad hurt, too?"

Hilary's mother stepped back and wiped her eyes on a tissue she pulled out of her pocket. "The doctor said that Brad's going to be all right. He's got a sprained arm, and he's scratched up a little. They're keeping him overnight for observation. But he'll be going home tomorrow." She paused, then said in a lower voice, "I'm afraid he blames himself for the accident, although the police say he did everything he could to avoid it." She sighed and shook her head. "I wish I knew why Amy went riding with him. She'd asked before, and I'd always said no. But I wasn't home, and I suppose she thought she'd be back before I realized she was gone. I'm sure she thought it was safe."

The corners of Mrs. Malone's mouth began to tremble. "Amy was so happy today," she whispered. "She and Brad are engaged, Mike. They'd just decided yesterday. There wasn't time to tell you."

Mr. Malone swallowed painfully, his eyes dark. "Engaged? Amy? Why, she's just a— She's not *old* enough to think about marriage!"

"She's grown up now," Hilary's mother said. There was a sharp, accusing edge in her voice, and she moved away from him. "You haven't seen her in a while. I don't suppose you've noticed."

Mr. Malone shook his head wonderingly. For the first time he seemed to see Hilary. He sat down beside her and stroked her face with one finger. His eyes searched hers intently. "How's my girl?" he whispered after a minute. "Are *you* all right?"

"Oh, Daddy," she cried, flinging her arms around his neck. "Daddy, it's so awful! I'm so sorry!" She wanted to say, "It's all my fault! I'm the one who made it happen!" But the words were all knotted up inside her, tied up with the tears that wouldn't come out.

Hilary's father pulled her close. "We're *all* sorry, baby," he said against her hair. "But we just have to have faith. We have to believe that Amy's going to be OK." Holding Hilary in the curve of his arm, he reached for Mrs. Malone's hand and pulled her down beside him. "Just *believe*, that's all," he said fiercely. For a long time they sat locked in silence. Hilary leaned against her father, her eyes closed, grateful for the warmth and strength of his arm. In spite of how she felt about him, having him there made it easier.

At last a door on the other side of the room opened, and a tall man wearing rumpled green hospital pants and a green smock came into the room. Hilary's mother got up, and her father stood, too, his arm around her shoulders.

"I'm Dr. Richardson," the man said wearily. "I've got some news, but I'm afraid it's not good."

Hilary couldn't help herself. "Amy's not going to die?" she cried, leaning forward in her chair.

"No, she's not going to die," Dr. Richardson said quietly, and Hilary fell back, limp and light-headed with relief. "But I'm afraid it looks as if the paralysis is serious," he added soberly. "We won't be able to tell the extent of it until we can run some more tests. But I must caution you that we believe at this time that it is permanent. It looks as though Amy won't be able to walk again."

"Oh, no!" Mrs. Malone whispered. She sagged against Hilary's father as if she were going to fall. "Oh, please, God, no!"

"There's a massive injury to the spine, between the seventh and eighth vertebrae," the doctor said. "There's also extensive nerve damage, but we won't know how much until we can do more tests and until the swelling goes down completely. That may take weeks, even months." He looked at his watch. "It's after eleven now, and Amy's heavily sedated and sleeping. There's nothing you can do here. I think you all ought to go home and get some rest. Tomorrow will come soon enough, and we'll know more then about the extent of her injuries."

"But I can't leave," Mrs. Malone said, her voice choked with tears. "I *have* to stay with her. What if—what if she should get worse or call for me in the night?" She turned to Hilary's father. "Mike, why don't you take Hilary home? You must be tired after coming all the way from Houston."

"No, I'm going to stay here with you," Mr. Malone said quietly. He looked down at Hilary's mother, his face lined with pain. "She's my daughter, too, and I love her, Meg, even if I haven't been around very much." He turned to Hilary. "Hilary, I want you to drive back to the island with Elena. We'll call you in the morning and let you know how Amy's doing."

Hilary nodded numbly. It was just like before. There were her mother and dad and Amy—and somewhere on the outside, she stood looking in. Only now there was an awful difference. Amy might never walk again. She and Brad might not to able to get married as they had planned. And it was all *her* fault.

Hilary hardly slept that night. The worst part, she thought afterward, was wanting to cry and not being able to. The tears just wouldn't come, even though there seemed to be a flood of them inside her, dammed up by emotions so complicated that she couldn't even name them. She woke up feeling more exhausted than when she'd gone to bed.

Elena had stayed overnight, and she called the hospital early in the morning. "There's no change." She sighed as she sat down at the table where Hilary had just poured a bowl of cereal. "The doctors are getting ready to do some tests, your father said. He'll call if there's any word." She paused. "Brad went home this morning. He's going to be just fine."

Hilary put down her spoon. Her cereal tasted like straw. "I want to go to the hospital," she said. "I want to see Amy." *I have to tell her how sorry I am,* she thought. *I have to tell her that I didn't mean what I said.*

Elena smiled somberly. "Sure. But let's wait until they're through with the tests. Anyway, I need to go over to the Pelican for a couple of hours. Want to come with me?" She looked closely at Hilary. "It'll help get your mind off things."

"No, thanks," Hilary said. "I just don't feel like it."

"Well, then, I'll come over about noon and drive you to the hospital. I'll have to go right back to the shop, but you can ride home with your mom and dad." Elena got up and bent over Hilary. "Try not to think about it, honey. And, please, you mustn't blame Brad. The police said he did everything he could to keep it from happening."

"Blame Brad?" Hilary looked up sharply. "How could I blame Brad? It wasn't *his* fault."

"I just thought—"

"It wasn't his fault because it was mine," Hilary said, and suddenly the words were tumbling out. "Amy and I were arguing, and Brad came over and asked her to go for a ride in his dune buggy. I butted in and told Amy not to go, and she got mad and decided to do it, just to spite me. And then I told her—I said—" The tears were bottled up inside her, choking her, and still she couldn't cry.

Elena pulled her chair closer and sat down, putting her arms around Hilary. "Oh, Hilary," she said compassionately. "You mean, all these hours you've been thinking that you're responsible?"

Hilary nodded. "It's the truth, Elena. I *am* responsible. If we hadn't argued and if I hadn't acted like such a know-it-all . . . Amy even *said* that she wouldn't have gone if I hadn't told her not to."

Elena spoke firmly. "I could tell you that you're wrong, but you probably wouldn't believe me. I could even say that Amy has always been stubborn and strong-willed and that she's always done exactly what *she* wanted to do, no matter what anybody else said. But right now, I don't think you'd really hear it." She sighed and stood up. "I guess this is something you'll just have to work out for yourself in your own way, Hilary. But the subject isn't closed. I'm here anytime you want to talk about it." She picked up her purse. "I'll be back around noon."

A half hour after Elena left, there was a knock on the door. It was Jason. Hilary clutched the knob and swallowed hard. Her heart was pounding so loudly she was sure he could hear it.

"Hilary, I just heard about what happened last night," Jason said as he came into the room. There was a worried frown on his face and a concerned expression in his eyes. "How's your sister?"

"They're doing more tests this morning," Hilary replied. She sat down on the sofa, and Jason took the chair opposite her. "Last night the doctor said that he thought Amy would be—permanently paralyzed." Hilary flattened out her voice, to keep it from trembling. "Brad—the guy who was driving the dune buggy—is OK. He was released this morning. Elena is coming over in a couple of hours, and we're going back to the hospital. Mom's there now, and Dad is, too. He—he's been living in Houston, but he came down last night."

Jason got up from his chair and knelt beside the sofa. "I'm awfully sorry about Amy," he whispered urgently. "I wish there were something I could do." In the silence, he reached for her hand. "If you want to cry, Hilary, go ahead. It never hurts, and sometimes it makes things better." Tentatively he reached out and smoothed the hair back from her forehead and then leaned forward, his arms going around her.

The touch of Jason's fingers, the warmth of his arms seemed to dissolve the bitter knots that had held back the tears, and Hilary leaned against him, sobbing. Jason held her tightly, his hand stroking her hair. After a long time she quieted, and Jason kissed her wet cheek and let her go.

"I want you to lie down," he said firmly. "You look absolutely washed out. I'll bet you didn't get any sleep last night."

Without protest, Hilary stretched out on the sofa, feeling warm and limp. She *was* tired, but it was a better kind of exhaustion than what she had felt that morning. Jason was right. It had been good to cry.

There was an afghan on the back of the sofa, and Jason unfolded it and tucked it around her. "I think you ought to sleep for a little while," he said. "How would you like to go out for a pizza tonight, after you get back from the hospital? I know you feel bad, but going out might help to take your mind off—"

Abruptly Hilary sat up. "Thanks," she cut

him off. "But I can't, not tonight. Maybe later." She wanted to go out with Jason—she wanted it more than she could say. But she couldn't let herself be happy with him when Amy lay so still and quiet. Especially when she knew that the accident was her fault. Everybody wanted her to get her mind off what had happened, but she knew that that was impossible. "I can't," she said again.

"OK. But I'm warning you, I don't take rejections very easily." Gently Jason pushed her back against the sofa cushions. "Now I think you ought to take a nap. When you wake up, you'll feel better." He leaned forward and kissed her lightly, on the lips. "Sleep now, Hilary."

And miraculously she did.

The blinds of Amy's hospital room were drawn against the bright noontime sun, and when Hilary came into the room, it took a few seconds for her eyes to adjust to the subdued light. Amy lay motionless in the bed, her golden hair lying limp and tangled across the pillow. She wore bandages on her bruised face and neck, and Hilary could see that she was badly cut and scratched. A bottle of colorless liquid hung suspended over one side of the bed, feeding into her arm through a needle. Hilary's mother and father were sitting quietly in the shadows, and Hilary saw with a start that they were holding hands. She looked quickly away, and her mother stood up and greeted her.

"Amy's been asking for you over and over, honey," she said with a hug. "She seems to want to tell you something."

"Hilary?" Amy's lashes were flickering, and her lips barely moved.

Hilary bent over the bed. "I'm here, Amy," she said tenderly, taking Amy's hand. "How do you feel?"

"I can't move my—legs," Amy said, her words slightly slurred. With an effort, she opened her eyes. "But I'm going to be OK. Please don't worry." Her voice faded, and Hilary could barely hear the last words.

Hilary tried to smile. "Don't worry?" she repeated. The antiseptic smell of the room floated over her in waves. "Well, of course we're going to worry, silly. We want you home again, just as soon as possible."

Amy nodded imperceptibly. She seemed to be trying to grasp Hilary's fingers, but she couldn't. Her eyes closed. "Are you sure?" she whispered weakly. "I haven't been very—" She paused. "You were right, Hilary, I shouldn't have . . ."

Hilary clutched her sister's hand. "No, Amy, *I'm* the one who—" Her stomach turned over.

"Listen, Amy, I didn't mean what I said," she whispered desperately. "You've got to believe me. You've got to forgive me!" But Amy's eyes were closed, and her hand hung limp.

Mr. Malone stood up and put his hand on Hilary's arm. "She's too tired to talk, honey," he said softly. "We'll let her sleep now. It's lunchtime. Why don't we go get something to eat while your mother stays with Amy?"

Reluctantly, Hilary let go of her sister's hand. What had Amy meant when she said she was sorry? *She* was the one who should be sorry, not Amy. She looked back. Amy's lashes were pale gold smudges against her white cheeks. Hilary blinked back the tears and followed her father out of the room and down the stairs to the hospital cafeteria.

"How about that table by the window?" Mr. Malone asked as they picked up their trays at the cashier's counter. The small cafeteria was full of hospital personnel wearing crisp white outfits, and Hilary felt conspicuous in her jeans and plaid blouse.

"OK," she said. They put their food on the table and sat down.

"It's good to see you again, Hilary," her father said, watching her intently. "How have you been?"

Hilary opened her carton of milk. "OK, I guess." She looked down at the tuna salad sandwich on her plate. Ever since her father had moved away, it had been awfully hard to talk with him. There was always so much she wanted to say, so much she wanted to share— the way she used to. But something always held her back, some undercurrent of resentment and anger that swirled inside her. She thought of what Elena had said about loving people for themselves, not because of what they did—or didn't do. If Elena was right . . .

"How about you?" she asked as casually as she could. "How have you been?"

Mr. Malone shrugged and picked up his sandwich. "Oh, I keep myself busy," he said with a slight grin, and his bright green eyes twinkled. "I've gotten a variety of new writing assignments over the past year, and I've been doing a substantial amount of traveling: New York, San Francisco, Mexico City."

"We noticed," Hilary said dryly. She picked up a potato chip. "Your letters are always about your trips to exotic places. Don't you ever stay at home anymore?"

"Sure. Actually, I like living in Houston. City life has a lot of advantages over life here on the island. South Padre is so far away from where things are happening." He munched a pickle thoughtfully. "And free-lance writing is certainly a lot more fun than working nine to five at the *Port Isabel Beacon.* I'm my own boss. I can make my own hours." He grinned wryly. "But to tell you the truth, even though my life may seem glamorous, it isn't exactly the fulfilling adventure I envisioned."

"With all that traveling, I suppose you don't have time to get lonely," Hilary said, not looking up. The next question was terribly important. "Do you have any—friends?"

"Yes, I have a few friends. But even with all the traveling, I still get lonely. To be honest, Hilary, I miss you and Amy—and your mother. Coming back reminds me of how awfully much I've missed you."

Suddenly angry, Hilary put down her fork. "How can you talk about *missing* us?" she hissed fiercely. "*You* were the one who decided to leave! And if you *really* missed us, you'd have come back home to the island a long time ago, wouldn't you?"

Mr. Malone looked at his daughter, his eyes dark. "I suppose you're right," he said after a minute. "But it's more complicated than that, Hilary. I've changed, your mom has changed—"

"Oh, don't think I'm asking you to come home," Hilary broke in hastily. She was surprised by the intensity of the feeling—was it resentment?—that welled up inside her. "We're getting along just fine without you."

Her father looked sad. "I'm sure you are," he said quietly.

Hilary continued as though he hadn't said anything. "It was really hard right after you left, because none of us understood why you were gone, not even Mom. But after a while we got used to it. In fact, it really doesn't matter at all anymore." She lifted her chin. "Mom's involved with the gallery and the shop, and I've got my painting, and Amy has a lot of friends. We're doing just fine." Suddenly she remembered Amy, lying paralyzed in the hospital bed upstairs. "Or we *were*, until—until—" Her voice broke, and she couldn't go on.

"I know." Her father reached for her hand across the table. "Your mother is doing a super job being an only parent to you and Amy. She and Elena have made a real success of the Pelican. And you girls seem happy and content."

"That's right," Hilary said bitterly, pulling her hand away. It wasn't fair of him to come back and pretend to be so concerned about them, just because of Amy's accident. She pushed her chair back. "It wasn't easy, especially for Mom. But now we've gotten used to getting along by ourselves. We kind of like it that way." She hesitated, thinking about her parents holding hands when she had walked into Amy's room. "Instead of being separated, why don't the two of you just get a divorce and have it over with? That would be better for everybody."

Her father sighed and got up. "I suppose so," he said tiredly. "Shall we go back upstairs and see if there's any news about this morning's tests?"

Chapter Seven

The test results, Hilary and her parents learned that afternoon, showed that Amy had suffered severe spinal damage.

"We can't tell just yet how extensive the permanent damage is because there is still so much swelling around the spinal column and the injured vertebrae," Dr. Richardson said as he showed them the X rays on the wall screen in his office. "We can't rule out the possibility of a partial recovery, I suppose, but I must tell you frankly that in all my experience, I've rarely seen a patient with this much damage recover enough to stand, much less walk." He sat down on the corner of his desk. "If I thought there was a real chance, I'd tell you so. But it's my opinion that Amy will be permanently paralyzed from the waist down." He smiled. "Considering the alternatives, we have a lot to be grateful for. She'll be confined to a wheelchair, of course, but otherwise she should be able to lead a perfectly normal life."

Hilary shut her eyes tightly against the sudden, dizzying pain that filled her. *A normal life?* She thought of the blue chiffon dress Amy had bought for the dance, with the matching blue shoes that she'd been so proud of. Now she would never wear the dress or the shoes, and she'd never dance again.

"When can she come home from the hospital, doctor?" Hilary's mother asked. Her voice was calm but her eyes were red rimmed, and her hands were clenched tightly in her lap.

Dr. Richardson shook his head and closed the file in his hand with a gesture of finality. "I'm afraid that question is premature, Mrs. Malone. Amy needs lots of rest and quiet, and we must do more tests before we can determine what kind of therapy should be prescribed for her. After she's well enough, we'll put her on a daily therapy program to strengthen her upper-body muscles and to reduce muscular deterioration below the waist. She'll also need regular counseling to help her deal with the inevitable problems that will arise as she adjusts to her physical constraints." He looked at them sympathetically. "I understand that she planned to be married."

Hilary's mother nodded. "She and Brad—the boy who was driving the dune buggy—hadn't set a date yet." She glanced at Mr. Malone. "They hadn't even had a chance to tell Amy's father yet."

"I'm sure that she'll be very troubled about her marriage plans," the doctor said. "Try to help her and Brad understand that if they do decide to marry, she'll be able to live normally, except for the wheelchair confinement. They can certainly go ahead with their plans, after a period of recuperation."

The doctor sounded so calm and matter-of-fact that Hilary stared at him in amazement. "But don't you see? This changes everything!" she burst out uncontrollably. If Amy couldn't walk, nothing would ever be the same again. "Amy and Brad—" She choked.

"If they care for each other, honey, they'll find a way to make it work," Hilary's father said gently. "And they'll be stronger because they worked it through together. The main thing is that she's alive." He picked up his wife's hand and held it tightly. "That's what we have to remember and be thankful for. She could easily have been killed."

Hilary swallowed. Yes, her father was right. She had to think of what *might* have happened and be grateful. But how could Brad continue to care about Amy, knowing she'd never walk again! And how could Amy live, knowing she'd never be able to swim or surf or run along the beach with her friends? She shook her head. Maybe her parents would get used to the idea, but she never would. And she didn't think Amy would either.

Outside the doctor's office, Hilary was surprised to see Brad waiting for them. He was wearing a bandage across his forehead, and one arm was in a sling. There were lines of worry around his mouth, and he looked pale and shaken. After he shook hands with Mr. Malone, he said, "How's Amy? Can I see her?"

Hilary's mother nodded. "They've given her something to make her sleep, Brad. But why don't you go look in on her. After she wakes up, she'll be awfully glad to know that you were here."

Some of the tension in Brad's face dissolved. "Gee, thanks, Mrs. Malone," he said gratefully. He paused and lowered his eyes. "Listen, I just want you to know how sorry I am," he said, his voice ragged. "I've been thinking about this every minute since the accident. I'm the one who's responsible for this whole thing. I mean, I knew you didn't want her to ride with me. If I hadn't bugged Amy, she would never have—"

Hilary drew in her breath sharply. Now was the time to tell everyone what had *really* happened, to get it off her chest. But just as she began to speak, her father broke in.

"Stop that, Brad. You're not to blame for the accident. The police say that the other driver pulled out in front of you and that you did everything you could to stop safely." He put his hand on Brad's shoulder. "I know how you must feel. But you can't accept the responsibility. Amy shouldn't have gone after her mother told her not to. The other driver should have been more careful about pulling out. And that's that. End of discussion."

Hilary swallowed. There was nothing she could say now.

Brad looked as though he might cry. "Thanks, Mr. Malone," he said thickly. "But just the same, I know I'm responsible. And whatever happens, I want you to know that this won't make any difference in the way I feel about Amy. She's a wonderful girl, and—" His voice broke, and he turned away, his shoulders shaking. "I'm sorry," he said after a moment. "It's all going to take some getting used to, I guess. If you don't mind, I'll go sit with Amy now."

"Well, Meg," Mr. Malone said thoughtfully, watching Brad walk away, "I still think Amy's too young to get married, and I hope they'll change their minds. But she seems to have made a pretty decent choice. Brad's acting like a mature young man." He put both hands on Mrs. Malone's shoulders and smiled wearily at her. "We're both pretty tired. Why don't we leave Hilary and Brad to stay with Amy this afternoon, and I'll drive you back to the island so you can get some sleep." He dropped his hands and stepped back. "I'll check into a motel, and we can come back over this evening after supper."

"If Brad's going to be here for a while, I think I'll go on back with you and Mom," Hilary said quickly. The thought of seeing Amy again, lying so still and helpless on the white sheets, was more than she could bear. Her mother gave her a questioning look, and she added lamely, "I think it would be better if Brad and Amy could be alone when she wakes up."

"Whatever you want, honey," Mrs. Malone said. She looked up at Hilary's father. "Mike, you're welcome to the spare bedroom. There's no point in going to the expense of a motel room, unless you just want to be by yourself." She smiled tentatively at Hilary. "I'm sure that Hilary would be glad to have her father close by for a while."

A numbing confusion rose up inside Hilary, and she remembered the resentment she had felt when she was having lunch with her father. Yes, she wanted to be with him. But wouldn't that just make it harder to bear when he left again? Was it fair to ask her to get used to having him around when she knew that it was just temporary? That he would go back to Houston in a few weeks, and she'd have to get used to losing him all over again? She looked at her mother, and after a long hesitation, she said, "Sure, I guess Dad can stay at the house, if that's what you want." But inside, she was crying out, *No, no, go away! I don't want to go through it all over again when you leave!*

"Well, then, the two of you have talked me into it," Mr. Malone replied cheerfully. He smiled at them. "I hope I won't be too much bother."

"No, no bother at all," Mrs. Malone replied. She shut her eyes briefly. "Could we go now? I didn't sleep much last night, and I'm awfully tired."

Mr. Malone put one arm around her shoulders and the other around Hilary's. "Come on, gang," he said. "Let's go—home."

For the next week or so, Hilary lost all sense of time. Every morning her parents would drive across the bridge to the hospital at Port Isabel to visit Amy. Every evening they would come back to the island, cook supper, and then one of them would go back again to the hospital. Hilary avoided going with them. Because Elena needed someone to replace Mrs. Malone in the shop, she had a good excuse not to go to the hospital during the daytime. But after a while she ran out of reasons not to visit her sister in the evening.

"Amy asked about you today," Mrs. Malone said as she and Hilary were finishing the supper dishes. Hilary's father had gone back to Houston to get his car and more clothes. He wouldn't be back until the next day. Hilary had come to look forward to the quiet evenings alone with her mother, cherishing them because when Amy came home, there would be *three* of them again, and she would have to go back to feeling left out.

Usually Mrs. Malone was tired from the long day at the hospital, and Hilary tried to do as much of the supper preparation and cleanup as she could. But in the last few days, she had noticed a sparkle in her mother's eyes and a pretty, rosy tint in her cheeks that hadn't been there for a long time. Hilary thought it was probably because Amy was doing better.

"Tell her that I think of her all the time," she said in reply to her mother's question. It was true. Always in her mind was the picture of Amy, still and quiet in the hospital bed. And in her ears was the echo of her own hateful words. "Just because I don't go to the hospital, doesn't mean that I don't think about her."

Her mother frowned. "She asked yesterday, too," she said quietly. "I think you should plan to go with me tomorrow evening, Hilary."

Hilary put away the last dish, folded the terry cloth towel carefully, and hung it up. How could she tell her mother that it was her guilt that kept her away? That she couldn't bear to see her sister lying motionless and pale, knowing that she was the one who was responsible for Amy's accident? And Amy knew it, too, which would make it even harder for both of them. "I—I've already made other plans," she lied, avoiding her mother's eyes. "Jason said he'd call me about going out tomorrow evening."

The part about Jason calling was true. In fact, he had called three times in the last few days to ask her to go out with him. But it wasn't true that they had made plans for the next evening. Hilary hadn't been able to bring herself to say yes to a date. If Brad and Amy couldn't be happy together, the way they had planned, how could she let herself be happy with Jason, even though she wanted desperately to see him—if only to confirm that he wanted to be with *her*.

The first two times he called and she had

said no, Jason hadn't seemed to mind. But that afternoon, when she had said she couldn't go for a walk on the dunes with him, there had been an unmistakable edge to his voice.

"Why don't you want to go out with me, Hilary?" he had demanded. "We had such a good time that day at Shell Beach, and you said you wanted to see me again. Remember? And when I came over to your house after the accident, I felt very close to you." He paused. In the silence Hilary remembered how his arms had felt around her, and she wondered if he were remembering the same thing. "What's happened?" he asked after a moment.

Hilary hung on to the telephone, flooded by a despair so intense that it made her dizzy. How could she answer him? What could she say that would make him understand? "Please, Jason," she whispered, "I really *do* want to see you. But this thing with Amy . . ."

There was another long pause. "I know it's been rough for you," Jason said quietly. "I'll call you again next week. But I'm putting you on notice, Hilary. I won't take no for an answer. OK?"

"OK," she had said weakly and hung up the phone. She felt like a condemned prisoner who had suddenly been given a reprieve.

"Well, I certainly understand that you want

to see Jason," Mrs. Malone was saying, "especially since the two of you were just getting acquainted when this thing happened. But I should think you'd want to see your sister, too, Hilary. The accident happened over a week ago, and so far you've only been to the hospital once. I wouldn't want Amy to think that you're avoiding—"

"Please, Mom," Hilary interrupted. "Tell her I—I love her and miss her. But I can't go to see her. I—I just can't." She knew she owed her mother more of an explanation than that, but she couldn't think of what to say.

Mrs. Malone gave her daughter a long, thoughtful look. "I think I understand, honey. It's pretty hard to see your sister lying there in bed, knowing that she can't walk." She paused. "But you really ought to visit her, no matter how difficult it is for you. She'll be home after a while, and you have to get used to her being in a wheelchair. She'll want to be as independent as she can, and we'll have to help her. If we all work together, things will work out right. But we've got to stick *together*."

Mutely, Hilary nodded. Her mother was right, but the guilt and anguish inside her wouldn't let her speak. How could things work out right if Amy were in a wheelchair for the rest of her life? Even though Brad didn't seem to be bothered by that right then, in a few weeks he would see that nothing was the same. And how could she be happy with Jason, knowing that Amy would never have that kind of happiness?

Her mother clicked off the light, and they went into the living room together. "Have you and your father had an opportunity to get reacquainted?" Mrs. Malone asked carefully as she sat down in a chair.

Hilary shook her head. She picked up a magazine from the stack on the coffee table and sat down on the sofa, leafing through it idly, to avoid her mother's gaze. "There really hasn't been any time," she said.

"Isn't that because you haven't *made* time?"

"I don't know what you mean."

"Of course you do, honey. Your dad thinks that you're avoiding him. He's afraid that you'd rather he went back to Houston, that you don't want him here." She paused. "Is that true, Hilary?"

Wearily, Hilary put down the magazine and shut her eyes. "I don't know. I just don't think it's fair to ask me to get 'reacquainted' with him when we both know that he'll be gone in a couple of weeks—maybe even a couple of days." She opened her eyes and looked at her mother and was startled to see that her mother didn't look at all upset by what she had just said. Hilary shut her eyes again. "I don't think it's fair for him to pretend that we're a family again, either," she said. "For one thing, it's not fair to you."

"I'm not worried about what's fair right now," Hilary's mother said carefully. She got up and came over to sit down beside Hilary. "I think it's important for your dad to feel like a part of the family. It won't hurt, will it, to help him just a little? After all, Hilary, he's your father. Your avoidance is very painful to him."

Hilary rested her head against her mother's shoulder, smelling her warm, flowery fragrance. She nodded reluctantly. "I guess you're right. I'll do what I can."

Her mother hugged her. "Thank you, Hilary," she whispered. "It's important for all of us." After a minute she spoke again. "Will you go to the hospital tomorrow?"

Slowly, painfully, Hilary nodded. Even though she dreaded it, there wasn't any way she could escape.

Amy was in the same hospital room, and the blinds were still pulled so that the room was shadowed and dark. The tubes were gone, however, and Amy was lying half propped up against the pillows, her eyes closed. Hilary followed her mother toward the bed, stomach churning, hands clammy. Hospital rooms had

105

such an awful *smell*, and she had the frightening feeling that she might be sick.

Mrs. Malone bent over the bed. "Hi, honey," she said brightly. "I've brought somebody to see you."

Amy's eyes opened. "Hilary?" she asked. Mrs. Malone nodded.

Hilary stepped forward. "Hello, Amy," she said uneasily. There was a metallic taste in her mouth. She swallowed, but it wouldn't go away.

Amy smiled slowly. The bandages were gone, and Hilary could see that the cuts on Amy's face and neck were healing. "I'm glad you came, Hilary," she said. "There's so much I . . ." Her voice faltered weakly, and she stopped. Tears gathered at the corners of her eyes and rolled slowly down her cheeks.

"I think I'll go downstairs for a cup of coffee and leave you two alone," Mrs. Malone said, turning toward the door. "I'm sure you've got a lot to talk about."

"No!" Panic-stricken, Hilary put her hand on her mother's arm. "Oh, no, please stay!" she said. "I mean, that is, I think you should stay so that we can all talk together." She tried to smile, feeling slightly dizzy. The antiseptic smell of the room was almost overpowering.

For a moment Mrs. Malone looked at her

worriedly. Then she said, "Of course, Hilary, if that's what you'd like."

She pulled out a chair, and Hilary sat down limply. There was an odd rushing sound in her ears, and she shook her head, trying to get rid of it.

"Well, Amy, how are you feeling today?" Mrs. Malone asked, going to the window to open the blinds slightly. She sat down in a chair on the other side of Amy's bed.

Amy turned her head away from the light. "A little better," she said. "The therapist came to see me this morning, and she says I can begin my exercises tomorrow. Once that happens, I should start feeling better." There was a determined set to Amy's mouth. "I'm really going to work hard on the exercises, Mom. I'm so tired of this bed!" She looked over at her sister. "Now, tell me what's happening at home, Hilary. Have you been over to the yacht club? Who's taking my shift in the dining room? Patty?"

Hilary shook her head and clasped her hands in her lap to keep them from trembling. "I don't know," she said in a small voice. "I haven't been over there since—since the accident." Lamely, feeling that she ought to say something more, she added, "Actually, I've been spending a lot of time at the Pelican lately. So I don't know much about what's going on anywhere else."

"Elena says that Hilary is terrific with the customers," Mrs. Malone reported proudly. She laughed a little. "Maybe I won't even have a job when it's time to go back to work."

"But you *must* be doing something else besides working, Hilary," Amy insisted. "Mom said something about your having a 'new interest,' but she wouldn't tell me who it was."

Remembering Amy's harsh skepticism the last time she had mentioned Jason, Hilary just shook her head. "Oh, there's nobody special," she said. Then, at her mother's quick, curious look, she went on in the lightest voice she could manage, "If something important happens in my love life, you'll be the first to know." She couldn't help adding a little bitterly, "I know how much you want me to start dating." The metallic taste seemed stronger now, and the rushing sound was louder.

"I've done some thinking about that," Amy said slowly. She gave Hilary a hesitant look. "Maybe I've been too pushy, Hilary. Your life is your own business. When you're ready to start dating, I'm sure you will." She turned to her mother, gesturing to the blanket over her knees. "Mom, it's really warm in here. Would you please fold back this blanket?"

"Sure, honey," Mrs. Malone got up and

folded the blanket and sheet to the foot of the bed.

Feeling sick with anticipation, Hilary forced herself to look. Amy was wearing pink, flowered shortie pajamas, and Hilary saw that her sister's tanned, bare legs were as beautiful as ever. Amy caught her gaze.

"You'd never know from looking at those fantastic legs that they aren't in good working order, would you?" she said teasingly. She stared down at herself and laughed a little. But her laugh trailed off into silence. "Silly, worthless legs," she said finally in a cramped voice.

Suddenly Hilary felt terribly sick. She stood up, swaying a little. "Mom," she whispered, "can you tell me where the bathroom is?"

Mrs. Malone pointed to a door in the corner of the room. "Right there," she said, starting to get up. "Can I do anything? You look awfully pale."

Hilary clutched the back of the chair to steady herself, her head spinning dizzily. The rushing in her ears turned to a roar. An icy black emptiness seemed to open up beneath her feet, and she felt herself falling to the floor.

After the fainting episode, Mrs. Malone didn't say any more about Hilary's going to the hospital to see Amy, and Hilary tried as best as she could to put the visit out of her mind. But the image of Amy's tanned legs stayed with her, as did the sound of her sister's voice saying, "Silly, worthless legs." If Hilary thought about it too much, she felt sick and faint all over again.

Two days after the hospital visit, Jason came over. He found Hilary sitting in a wicker chair on the deck, looking out to the west, over the lagoon. "I took a chance you'd be here," he said. "I didn't want to get turned down again, so I didn't call."

Hilary couldn't look at him. "I'm sorry," she said lamely. "I've been working all day at the shop, and there just hasn't been time for—" She shivered. It was late afternoon, but the sun was hidden behind a bank of gray clouds, and the breeze was cool.

"I didn't come to talk about that," Jason said calmly. "I came to tell you that I'll be away for a few weeks. My parents and I are going up to Dallas to visit my aunt and uncle." He turned to face her, and there was a look in his eyes that made Hilary feel warm in spite of the cool breeze. "I hate to leave, Hilary. There's something good trying to happen between the two of us."

Hilary felt as though her face were tightening up. "I hope you have a good time in Dallas," she said stiffly. There was so much more she wanted to say, but that was all she could manage. Her feelings were tangled. She didn't want Jason to leave, but at the same time she was relieved that he was going. Now she wouldn't have to keep saying no—maybe to the point when he wouldn't even ask anymore.

Jason stood up, unsmiling. "Please let it happen, Hilary," he said as if she hadn't spoken. He put his hand on the back of her neck.

"Have a good time," she repeated carefully, not looking up. She ran her hand along the side of the chair, watching her fingers curl around the wicker arm.

"I'll try." For an instant Jason lingered, his hand warm and heavy on her neck. And then he left. For a long time Hilary sat shivering, staring out at the gray water.

One evening a week later, when it was her mother's turn to go to the hospital, Hilary and her father collaborated on a big pot of beef stew, one of Hilary's favorite meals. After her talk with her mother, Hilary had tried to be more affectionate toward her father, even though it felt forced and fumbling. But her efforts seemed to be having some effect. He was looking more like his old self, and she was beginning to feel much more comfortable with him.

When supper was over and the dishes were washed, her father said, "How about walking up to the dunes to watch the sun set over the lagoon?" He grinned. "We can take the binoculars and see who can identify the most birds."

Hilary felt a momentary pang. It was a game they had often played before her father moved away. But she agreed to go.

The sun was nearly setting when they got to the top of the tallest dune, and the sky was stained with red and gold. It was a lovely evening, and they spent fifteen or twenty minutes watching the birds feed in the shallow waters of the lagoon. There was something healing about the companionable silence, and Hilary felt better than she had in a long time.

"Hey, look! There's a white ibis!" she said excitedly, pointing to the tidal flat below them. "That's the first one I've seen all year."

Her father reached for the binoculars. "And isn't that a great blue heron?" he asked. "Over there to the right?"

"Can't you identify that one without the binoculars?" Hilary teased. "You're getting rusty."

Mr. Malone grinned. "You'll have to admit that there aren't many great blue herons walking the streets of Houston," he retorted. "But I guess I am a little out of practice." He handed

112

the binoculars back to Hilary and sat down on a gnarled gray stump. "I haven't seen any of your watercolors yet, Hilary. Elena says you're coming along very well. She says you've got real talent. What do you think?"

Hilary sat down in the sand beside him and thought regretfully about the work she had planned to enter in the art festival. "I don't know. I guess so. I was happy with what I was doing before Amy's accident. But there hasn't been much time to paint in the last couple of weeks." Below them a small brown plover darted along the sand, and Hilary picked up the binoculars to watch it feed. Through the glasses, she could see that it had a collar of dark feathers around its neck. "Maybe there'll be more time later this summer."

Mr. Malone looked down at her. "Well, don't put it off too long, honey. If you wait to do the things you want, they might not turn out the way you thought they were going to. And then you'll be disappointed."

Hilary nodded, thinking about Jason. How much longer would he take no for an answer? Below her, the plover was joined by two others, and the three splashed enthusiastically in the quiet water, obviously having found a school of small fish.

There was a long silence. Finally Mr. Malone

cleared his throat. "Hilary, there's something I want to tell you."

Suddenly a white herring gull dive-bombed the plovers. They scattered frantically, and the greedy gull began to enjoy their feeding grounds in splendid isolation. Hilary put down the binoculars, still thinking of Jason. "What is it?" she asked absently.

"Amy's accident was a terrible thing," Mr. Malone said, "but it's brought about something very good, at least as far as your mother and I are concerned." Slowly he traced circles in the sand with his fingertips.

Hilary clasped her arms around her bent knees. For a moment, watching the birds in the golden twilight, she had forgotten about Amy. "Good?" she whispered bitterly. She pressed her forehead against her knees, hearing the echo of Amy's words in her ears. "What possible good could it have brought?"

Her father continued to draw circles, not looking at her. "Hilary, before Amy's accident your mother and I had planned to file for a divorce this summer. But now we feel very differently. We've decided to get back together again." He drew a deep breath. "Both of us hope you'll be happy about it."

Stunned, Hilary sat still, hardly breathing, while the twilight darkened around them and even the herring gull flew away. "I—I don't know what to say," she replied at last. Her voice sounded very small in the silence.

"Can't you say you're happy?"

Hilary shook her head. "I don't know," she said truthfully. "I mean, I thought for a long time that this was exactly what I wanted." She looked up at her father. "For a long time I *prayed* that you would come back."

"And now?"

"And now I just don't know. I guess I'm glad for you and Mom. If it's what you two want. But I'm not sure about me." Hilary's throat hurt, and tears stung her eyes. She began to rock back and forth, arms still clasped around her legs. "I mean, you've been gone for so long. You decided to leave us, and I had no choice but to get used to it. And now, just because you decide to come back again, you expect me to get used to it again. I don't see how things can ever be the same."

Mr. Malone nodded. "You're right; they can't. But the truth is, I don't expect them to be. At least, not in the way I think you mean. There were lots of things wrong, before. I wouldn't *want* us to go back to being the way we were." He smiled down at her a little sadly. "I wouldn't blame you if you didn't trust me, Hilary. Maybe you think that the same thing will happen again, later on. But people *do* change, you know. A year ago, I thought I wanted a brand-new life of my own, independent of my family. A glamorous, exciting life with lots of travel and time alone to write. Now I know how empty and lonely that kind of life can be. I want us to be a family again. And your mom is willing to try." He put his arms around Hilary's shoulders and drew her against him. "Will you try, too?" he whispered.

Hilary pulled away. She wanted to say yes, but she couldn't. She wanted to throw her arms around him and cry with happiness, but she couldn't. Her father was right. She didn't trust him—or her own feelings, for that matter. "I guess so," she said finally in a flat, dull voice. It was the best she could do.

Her father dropped his arm and stood up. "I guess it's too soon, honey," he said. "It'll take some time for you to get used to the idea. Let's talk again, later, after you've thought about it."

They walked back down the beach to the house in silence. But it wasn't the kind of comfortable silence they'd shared before, and Hilary felt as if she'd found something precious only to lose it again.

Chapter Eight

The next week seemed to drag by painfully and slowly. Hilary spent most of the day at the shop, helping Elena, a job that she began to treasure because it kept her mind off Amy and her parents—and off Jason, who was still in Dallas. With Amy in the hospital, Hilary really wanted to spend more time with her mother, and she had looked forward to their evenings together alone. But since her parents' reconciliation, her mother and father seemed to be completely wrapped up in each other. Hilary could *understand* how they felt, but she found it hard to accept. So, for the most part, she tried to stay away from them. When they were all together, she couldn't help but feel excluded and more than a little envious of their private happiness. But Hilary could also see that her parents' new pleasure in each other was marred by their terrible uncertainty about Amy's condition.

Mr. and Mrs. Malone were both at the hospital most of the day, and when they came home, they brought reports of Amy's progress, sometimes discouraging, sometimes encouraging. She had started therapy now, and even though the going was slow and painful, she seemed to be doing well. She was in a wheelchair, and they were expecting to bring her home for a short visit before long. Of course, even after she was home to stay, there would be daily trips to the hospital for continued therapy.

One evening when her father had gone to visit Amy, Mrs. Malone came into Hilary's room. Hilary was curled up on the window seat reading a book, with Missy on her lap. "We haven't had much time to talk in the last week," Mrs. Malone said, sitting on the bed.

"I know," Hilary replied, turning a page. "You and Dad have been awfully busy, and I've been at the shop all day. There hasn't been much free time."

"But you've been avoiding us," her mother pointed out gently. "You seem to prefer being alone. What is it, Hilary? Are you still upset about Amy? Or are you unhappy about Dad's coming back?"

Hilary put down her book. She didn't want to talk about her father or her feelings about the reconciliation. It was safer to talk about Amy, even though the burden of responsibility for Amy's accident weighed heavier on her mind every day.

"Well, it's not easy to accept the idea that Amy—isn't going to walk again," she said finally. She stroked Missy's soft striped coat, and the cat snuggled into the curve of her arm, purring loudly. She wanted to add, "Especially when I know it's my fault," but she didn't.

Mrs. Malone looked thoughtful. "You know, I'm not sure any of us *should* accept that idea," she said. "Amy doesn't seem to have accepted it. The therapist has assigned her a very demanding set of exercises, and she's supposed to do them four hours a day. But she does almost *twice* that much, and she seems to be getting stronger faster than anyone had expected." There was a smile in her eyes. "Hilary, I know how upset you were at seeing your sister in the hospital, and I understand why you fainted. That's why I haven't pressed you to visit her again. But I think you should see her now. She has changed a great deal through all of this, and I don't mean physically."

"Changed?"

Hilary knew she must have looked skeptical because her mother said, "Wait until you see her before you make any judgments." She smiled mysteriously. "Anyway, even though Dr. Richardson still thinks the paralysis is probably permanent, Amy is absolutely determined to prove him wrong. And I'm glad she has such a positive attitude." She got up and walked over to the window seat and put her hand on Hilary's shoulder. "But that's not all that's bothering you, is it, Hilary? Does it have something to do with Dad and me?"

Hilary still didn't want to talk about her father, but it looked as though she couldn't avoid the subject. "I don't know what to think about his coming home," she confessed, looking out the window as the Port Isabel beacon began its nightly pendulum swing across the water. "I was angry when Dad left, and I thought I wanted him to come home more than anything else. But now I'm not sure. How can we know that he's changed? That he really wants to be with us?"

"We can't *know* something like that," Mrs. Malone said. She bent over and rested her cheek against Hilary's hair. "We just have to trust one another, Hilary. Believe in one another, in the same way that we have to believe that Amy's going to have a happy life, whether she walks again or not."

Hilary was silent for a moment. "Are *you* happy about Dad?" she asked at last. "Are you glad to have him here?"

"Yes," her mother replied softly. "I'm *very* glad. I think we're both where we belong— together. But I'd be much happier if I knew that you felt good about it, too."

Hilary turned and put her arms around her mother's waist. She couldn't bring herself to complain about feeling left out, even though the feeling was very real. "I'll try," she said, burying her face against her mother's shoulder. "But it may take some time."

"I understand," Mrs. Malone said gently. She stroked her daughter's hair. "Will you visit Amy tomorrow evening? I want you to see how much she's changed."

Numbly, Hilary nodded, thinking about what had happened the last time.

"Good." Her mother hugged her hard. "She'll be awfully glad to see you."

Amy had been moved to a room in a bright, cheerful ward with five other beds that were separated from one another by white screens. But Amy's cubicle was different. Her pink-flowered spread was folded at the foot of the hospital bed, and an oversize Garfield poster grinned from the wall, surrounded by a flock of colorful get-well cards. The last time Hilary had arrived empty-handed. But that day she had brought a vase filled with wild flowers and grasses from the dunes, which she set on the nightstand beside Amy's bed. She swallowed down the faint queasiness that rose in her throat and turned toward her sister.

"Oh, Hilary, I'm so glad you've come!" Amy exclaimed. "I've *missed* you!"

Hilary gaped at her sister. Amy's voice was so warm and welcoming. But what really astonished Hilary was Amy's hair! It had been cut short, almost like a boy's, and it made her face look entirely different, emphasizing her wide cheekbones and the firm lines of her jaw. Amy was sitting up in bed against a pile of pillows, wearing pretty pink pajamas. Brad was there, too, perched on the edge of the bed, holding her hand.

"I—I'm sorry about last time," Hilary said hesitantly.

Amy looked concerned. "Mom said she thought you were just working too hard. I hope you're feeling better."

"Oh, much," Hilary replied, grateful for her mother's white lie. She stared at her sister. Amy looked much stronger than she had the last time—and somehow, incomprehensibly, even stronger than she had *before* the accident! Was this the change her mother had referred to?

Amy gestured toward an empty chair at the side of the bed. "I'll bet Elena can't get along without you, especially with Mom spending so much of her time here."

"Well, it's sort of fun," Hilary said, sitting on the edge of the chair. Briefly she puzzled over the indefinable difference in her sister. She could see that Amy had lost weight. She looked—well—older and more mature, somehow. Hilary decided that she really liked Amy's new haircut, and she told her sister so. "I hope you'll be home soon," she added, trying to think of something neutral to say. There was so much on her mind, but with Brad listening, she couldn't really share her thoughts with Amy.

"The doctor says maybe next week," Brad said. "It can't be too soon, as far as I'm concerned." He squeezed Amy's hand. "This hospital is for the birds. I want my girl back home, where I can see her whenever I want to, without some grouchy nurse telling me that visiting hours are over. Where I can help take care of her."

Amy glanced impatiently at Brad. "But I don't *need* people taking care of me," she objected.

Brad patted her hand. "That's OK, honey," he said gently. "You just relax and get well."

Amy shook her head and smiled at Hilary. "You and I have a lot of talking to do," she said quietly. "Being cooped up here has given me lots of time to think about the way we've acted toward each other. Or at least about the way *I've* acted." She looked at Hilary carefully as though she were waiting to measure her sister's response.

Amy's words and her direct gaze caught Hilary off guard, and she looked away. Her glance caught the empty wheelchair by the side of the bed. Suddenly her heart felt as though it were being tied into knots, and all the queasiness came back in a rush. "I've thought about it, too," she said painfully. "In fact, I—I haven't been able to think about much of anything else." There was a long pause, then she burst out, "Oh, Amy, I'm so sorry!" She leaned forward, reaching for her sister. "It was all my—"

Amy threw her a warning look, with a slight shake of her head toward Brad. "Let's talk later," she said. "When I'm at home and we have plenty of time to spend together."

Brad threw back his head and laughed heartily. "When you two girls spend time together, you don't talk—you fight," he said, teasing. "Let's face it. You'll never change.

It's a fifteen-round championship boxing match whenever you're together for more than two minutes."

Amy shook her head. "No, that's all over," she said firmly. "A lot of things have changed in my life, and I—" She looked at Brad and stopped abruptly, then turned to her sister. "Speaking of changes, Hilary, what do you think about Dad and Mom getting back together again? Isn't it wonderful?"

Hilary managed a smile. "Well, Mom certainly seems happy," she answered evasively. She had seen her parents from her window that morning, coming back from an early walk along the beach. They were barefoot and holding hands and giggling like—well—like teenagers. Watching them had given her a funny feeling, as though she were spying, and she had hastily closed the curtains.

"Dad has been acting like a kid," Amy said with a laugh. "This morning when they were here, he snuck a kiss from Mom, and she actually blushed." She paused, looking a little doubtful. "I hope you're feeling OK about it now, Hilary. Dad said you had some reservations."

"I just said I didn't quite understand it, that's all," Hilary replied defensively. "I love Dad, and I guess I'm glad to have him back. I'm just not sure—" She stopped. What wasn't she sure about? That he might leave again? Or that he might stay?

"I know," Amy said soothingly. "I was worried, too, in the beginning. I kept thinking about how Mom would feel if he decided to leave again. But Mom seems to be willing to take that risk."

"It looks like a good thing to me," Brad observed approvingly. He stood up and stretched. "Especially since your mom's going to be by herself pretty soon. After all, you have only one more year of high school, Hilary, and then you'll probably go away to college—right? And"—he turned to Amy—"we're getting married sometime next year." Tenderly, he put his arm around her shoulders and smiled down at her. "Then I'll *really* be able to take care of you."

"I've told you, Brad, we're not getting married until I can take care of myself," Amy said defiantly. She glanced at the wheelchair and wrinkled her nose in distaste. "I certainly don't plan to stay in that thing forever. But even if I *have* to use it to get around, I'm *still* going to be independent!"

Brad looked doubtful. "I don't know, Amy," he said. "I don't think you ought to push yourself so hard. Those exercises you're doing, for instance. You don't have to try to get well all at once, do you? Just take it slow and—"

Amy made a face at him. "But if I take it slow, I'll *never* get well. You heard what Dr. Richardson said—if I can keep the muscles from deteriorating, I'll have a much better chance."

She turned to Hilary, changing the subject again. "What do you think? Will Dad go back to his old job at the *Beacon*? Or will he want us to move to Houston, where he can keep doing his free-lance writing?"

Startled, Hilary looked at Amy, her eyes widening. Move to Houston? She had been so caught up in her confusion about her father's return that she hadn't even thought about the future. Wouldn't her parents want to stay on the island? They *couldn't* leave, could they, considering Amy's situation? And even if Amy and Brad got married later on, wouldn't her mom want to stay close by where she could help?

Hilary swallowed the hard, stinging lump that had suddenly stuck in her throat. What would *she* do if her parents decided to move? It would mean leaving the island and the seashore and the beautiful dunes. But even more important, it would mean leaving Jason— before she had a chance to find out if what was between them was important and lasting! Suddenly the world seemed infinitely more complicated and confusing than it had been just a few minutes before.

The next day was Saturday, and Elena had gotten a temporary helper and given Hilary the day off as a reward for her hard work over the last several weeks. After her parents had left for the hospital, Hilary packed up her painting gear and headed up toward Shell Beach. The sky was gray and overcast, and the flat ocean swells were silvery, reflecting the leaden color of the clouds. Hilary felt tired, and the walk up the beach didn't seem to be as much fun as usual. The tide was very low and the beach was covered by a brownish-green, smelly seaweed that made Hilary wrinkle her nose in distaste. To make matters worse, some careless campers had left an ugly trail of beer cans and paper along the sand. Even the birds seemed unhappy about it, and they circled over the waves, far from the shore, cackling disdainfully.

At Shell Beach Hilary collected a mound of interesting shells and driftwood, selected several of the best pieces for an arrangement, and began to paint. But nothing seemed to come out the way she wanted it to. The colors seemed muddy and dull, the shapes were uninteresting, and the texture was flat and lifeless. She stared at the watercolor for a long moment. It looked just the way she felt—dull and spiritless.

After several more unsatisfactory attempts, she gave up and sat down on a cypress log and ate the sandwich she had packed. *If only Jason were here,* she thought. *He might be able to point out something I could do to improve this stuff.* But it wasn't help with her painting that she wanted most from Jason, she reflected. She just wanted to be *with* him, to know that he cared about her. She sighed and propped her chin in her hand, thinking about what Amy had said the night before. If her mother and father decided to move to Houston, she would never see Jason again. A wave of desperate unhappiness swept over her.

"Well, Merriweather, if it ain't Jason's friend," a gritty cheerful voice said from the top of a nearby dune. "Hello, there, Miss Hilary."

Hilary looked up. A man was silhouetted against the sky, a dog at his knee. "Hello, Sam," she said, happy to be distracted from her thoughts. Merriweather began to bark enthusiastically.

"I came to see if last night's high tide brought in any nice hunks of whittling wood," Sam said, scrambling down the dune. He was wearing his captain's hat, and he had a pipe clenched firmly in his teeth. "I didn't know I'd find you here." He looked at her with curiosity. "It looks like you might be doing some pretty heavy thinking. Am I butting into something private?"

Hilary shook her head. "No, not at all," she said. "I was just trying to decide what's wrong with my watercolors. They aren't coming along so well." She looked around. "I think I saw a piece of driftwood that might be what you want." She spied it and went to pick it up. It was a chunk of dark, salt-stained wood, about the shape of her tennis shoe but unexpectedly heavy for its size. Sam's eyes lit up when he saw it.

"Well, I'll be durned," he said. "That little beauty sure has swum a long ways. We don't grow them like that anywhere close by."

"What kind of wood is it?" Hilary asked curiously. She rubbed her finger along the grain and saw that the wood had a deep, satiny sheen.

"This here's a piece of mahogany, come all the way up from the British Honduras," Sam said, taking the driftwood from Hilary and hefting it. "A long time ago it was probably part of a giant tree that was knocked over in a hurricane. Or maybe it just gave in to the waves and the winds that kept pounding away at it year in and year out. No telling how long the currents have floated it around, or where else it's been."

Sam turned the driftwood over in his hands. "You know, every living thing has a past, and it ain't always what you'd expect. Take this piece of wood, for instance. First it's a tree, growing on some deserted beach where nobody but the birds can see it or appreciate it. Then some big storm comes ripping along and wipes out the tree. And this here hunk of wood goes for a long swim around the Caribbean, behaving like a regular fish, getting acquainted with the dolphins and the starfish and the coral reefs and the beaches. And now it's about to start life all over again—as a pretty little bird."

He looked around, and a sandpiper, dipping gracefully into the surf, caught his eye. "See that little feller over there? I'll bet this here piece of mahogany would just love to grow up to be a sandpiper." He grinned at Hilary. "Seems fitting, don't it? First a tree, then a fish, and then a bird."

Hilary laughed. It seemed strange to think about a piece of wood being a fish or a bird. Wood was wood. Even if Sam carved it into a bird, that was still the same thing, wasn't it?

"Well, now, little lady, you wouldn't laugh if you knew the truth of things," Sam said mildly. He took the pipe out of his mouth and sat down on the log. Hilary sat down beside him, and Merriweather lay her head against her knee. "Everything's got to change. That's part of life, ain't it? Take old Pat, for instance. Why, that old boat wouldn't ever have guessed that someday she'd be content to leave the Gulf and be moored on a dune, would she? But now that she's there, with me and Merriweather to live with her and take care of her, she's happy as a clam."

Sam puffed on his pipe for a moment, absently rubbing his thumb against the piece of mahogany he held in his lap. "Changing and adapting," he said finally. "That's the secret of survival—and the secret of being happy. Learn to live with what comes along. A boat gets a chance to be a fine, cozy house. A tree gets a chance to uproot itself and be a bird." He looked at Hilary, and his watery blue eyes were warm. "And an old sea captain gets to be a spinner of tall tales," he said, standing up. "Guess I owe you something, little lady. This here's a mighty fine piece of wood."

Hilary shook her head. "No, I'm the one who owes something, Sam. Thanks for the talk."

After Sam had gone, Hilary packed up her gear, wrapping her watercolors carefully, and started back down the beach. *"Everything's got to change,"* Sam had said. *"That's part of life."* She thought of the mahogany tree, knocked down by the hurricane and battered by the Gulf currents, now about to start a new life under Sam's talented hands. She thought about Amy, determined to defy her doctor and walk again. She thought of her father, wanting to have his own life, separate from his family's—and then discovering the loneliness that that could bring. And her mother, adapting to the separation and learning to live with what came along. Changing and adapting. She lifted her chin. The sun had come out, and the waters of the Gulf had turned blue and sparkling. When she got home she would call and find out whether or not Jason was back from Dallas. Suddenly it seemed to her that phoning him was exactly the right thing to do.

Chapter Nine

"I'm really glad you called this afternoon," Jason said as they walked into the Village Pizza Parlor. "But I'll have to admit that it was a surprise." He stepped up to the counter. "What do you want on your pizza?" he asked.

"Everything," Hilary said. And then added hastily, "Except anchovies."

"OK, everything except anchovies," Jason said to the woman behind the cash register. "And two of the biggest, coldest root beers you've got." He smiled at Hilary. "This is a celebration."

The pizza parlor was usually crowded with tourists, but that night it was almost deserted. Hilary and Jason carried their root beers to a quiet corner with a window overlooking a rocky jetty that jutted out into the ocean. The sun was low in the sky, and the surf that curled over the granite boulders looked as though it had been brushed with gold. "In a way, it was a surprise to me, too," Hilary said frankly. She had been nervous when she dialed Jason's number, but she had known that it was the right thing to do, and she was glad that he had answered her with an enthusiastic yes when she had asked him to go for a pizza.

"So what *did* make you decide to call?" Jason asked when they were settled. He was wearing a light yellow tennis shirt, open at the throat, and his tan showed dark against the pale color.

Hilary considered. Should she give him an evasive answer, or should she tell him the truth? Amy would probably have invented some cute, silly reason that would make him laugh. Hilary took a deep breath. She didn't want to hide *anything* from Jason, even if she had to run the risk of being too serious. "I said no before because I—I was so upset about Amy," she said. "Just before the accident, we had a big argument. Amy and Brad had decided to get married, and I told her I thought she was too young. The next day when Brad drove up in his dune buggy and asked her to go for a ride, we were still arguing. I—I said some things I shouldn't have. The truth is that Amy wouldn't have gone with Brad if I hadn't reminded her that Mom had told her not to. She did it just to show me that I couldn't tell her what to do. She said as much, just before she took off." Hilary couldn't meet Jason's eyes. "So you see, I'm the one who's responsible for the accident."

"And because Amy got hurt, you decided to punish yourself by not going out with me?" Jason asked. The tone of his voice was slightly ironic, but his blue eyes were sympathetic.

"Well, I guess you could put it that way," Hilary said hesitantly. "How could I have any fun, if Amy couldn't? And especially when it was my fault that she was in the hospital."

"I don't believe for one minute that you're responsible for Amy's accident," Jason said firmly. "And you still haven't explained why you called today."

"I'm not sure I *can* explain," Hilary said slowly. "It has something to do with Sam. I met him up at Shell Beach today." She tipped her mug and watched the root beer foam against the frosty glass. Then she told Jason Sam's story about the boat that became a house and the tree that became a bird. "What Sam said about changing and adapting made me think. So many things have happened this summer. I guess I have to learn to adapt. And I have to believe that something good is going to come from Amy's accident." She thought again of Amy's beautiful, useless legs, and she shivered. "I know that it sounds kind of strange. But when you think about it, there's something to Sam's story." She looked intently at Jason. It was very important that he understand. "Before that piece of mahogany driftwood could be carved into a beautiful bird, something terrible had to happen to the tree. Do you see?"

Jason nodded, not taking his eyes off hers. "That's Sam for you. He calls his stories tall tales, but every one of them's got a message, and sometimes the messages are pretty important." He reached for her hand, and his fingers were cool and firm against her palm. "How's Amy?" he asked. "And your mom? The last month must have been pretty terrible for everybody in your family. It's no wonder you find it hard to believe that any good could possibly come from it. But who knows. Maybe something will."

Hilary relaxed in her chair. Jason *had* understood. She felt better immediately. "Amy's already talking about being independent, although Brad wants her to just let him take care of her," she said, remembering the conversation in the hospital room. "She's even talking about walking! Dr. Richardson doesn't seem very optimistic, but she's working hard on her therapy program. That's a big change. Amy never worked hard at anything before." She dropped her eyes. "And there's a big change at home, too. My parents have been separated for a year. But now Dad's come home, and my mom's very happy." She hesitated. "They all seem to be adapting."

Jason whistled softly. "Sounds as if they've all been going through some pretty heavy changes." He leaned across the table. "And how about Hilary?"

Hilary looked out the window, where the gold was beginning to fade from the crests of the waves. "Hilary's surviving," she said simply.

"Just surviving?" Jason asked. His fingers closed over hers. "Isn't there more to it than that? Aren't you enjoying your work at the shop? And how's your painting coming along? The art festival isn't far off, you know; entries are due on August tenth."

Jason's hand on hers felt very right. "I really like working at the shop, and I'm getting pretty good at it, too," Hilary answered. "Elena promised I could help with inventory next week because I know where everything is." She paused uncomfortably, thinking about his second question, but she had to be truthful. "As far as my painting's concerned, I'm afraid I really haven't felt much like working. And when I finally *make* myself paint, I'm not very happy with what I've done." She sighed as she thought of her morning's work, up at Shell Beach. "So I guess I'm not going to enter anything in the festival after all."

Jason frowned. "You know, you can't put off painting until you feel good. Sometimes I do my best work when I'm feeling lousy. There's room for all kinds of emotions in art, you know, not just happy ones." He looked as if he were about to say something more, but the waitress brought their pizza to them, and they talked of other things while they ate and watched the ocean turn to a soft, indistinct gray.

The moon was already beginning to cast silvery shadows as Jason and Hilary walked slowly along the lane that led to the Malone's house. Jason was telling her about the two oil paintings he planned to enter in the festival. "One is a painting of the *Princess Pat*," he said, "with Merriweather standing in the bow, wearing her red bandanna and Sam's hat and scanning the horizon for possible sharks. I've called it *Watch Dog*."

Hilary giggled. "Sounds like a real winner!

But how did you get Merriweather to hold still long enough to get a good sketch of her?"

"Oh, I didn't," Jason said. "I worked from color photographs I took of her the time before you and I were up there. That's why I carry my camera wherever I go. It helps me capture details—and it's great for studying reluctant subjects who don't want to hold still for me."

"Tell me about your second painting. Is it a seascape?"

"It's a secret—but you'll see it soon enough. And I guarantee that you'll like it." He turned toward her, his face a pale blur in the dark. "You know, it would be a real shame if you didn't enter something in the festival, Hilary. If you don't have anything else, you could enter the watercolors you did that morning up at Shell Beach. I liked them, and I think they're good enough to win a prize."

"Well, I'm not so sure," Hilary said doubtfully. "They're the best things I've done, but I'd have to mat and frame them first. And that's a lot of work."

"Well, sure, but you'd have to do that with anything you entered," Jason pointed out. "Anyway, I bet Elena will let you use the matting tools at the shop, and I'll help." He took her hand. "Maybe in the meantime, you can get started on something else. In fact, since tomorrow's Sunday, I'd planned to hike up to Sam's place in the afternoon and take a few more pictures of his boat and one or two of Merriweather. I'd rather go in the morning, but my mom's got some things for me to do around the house. Maybe you'd like to bring your painting gear and come along. We could stop at Shell Beach for a while and go swimming."

"I'd love to go with you," Hilary said promptly. "While we're there, I'd like to make some sketches of Sam's woodcarvings, and maybe one or two quick watercolor studies." The rich texture of the wood and the graceful shapes of the birds would be a real challenge for her, and if the work turned out well, maybe she could enter it in the festival.

"OK, I'll come over about one o'clock," Jason said with satisfaction. "That'll give us plenty of time to get back before dinner."

Regretfully, Hilary realized that they had reached the foot of the stairs that led up to her house. What did people say when they came back from a date with somebody they liked a lot? "Thanks for the pizza," she offered hesitantly, not knowing what else to say. "I had fun." The words sounded lame and inadequate. There was so much more in her heart.

"Thank *you*," Jason replied and put an arm

around her waist. Gently he pulled her toward him. "I've wanted to kiss you—*really* kiss you—ever since that first night," he whispered, putting his other arm around her waist. "Remember? The night that you got mad at me and tore up your watercolor."

Without a word, Hilary lifted her lips, and he brought his down on hers, gently, tenderly. His arms tightened around her, and Hilary could feel her pulse quicken and a trembling excitement surge through her in a warm wave. Longingly, she wished that the kiss would never end. But at last they broke apart.

"Does that mean you're not mad at me anymore?" Jason asked teasingly. He traced the outline of her cheek lightly with his finger. "Hilary, you know something? You're a very pretty girl. And right now, with the moonlight on your face, you're beautiful." He smiled, and Hilary's heart turned over. "I'd love to do a portrait of you, just as you look right now."

Hilary rested her forehead against his shoulder. "Thank you," she whispered, her words muffled by his shirt. She was trembling. No boy had ever kissed her or told her before that she was pretty.

"I asked you once before if I could do your portrait, but you said no," Jason reminded her, gently tipping up her face with one hand so that she had to look at him. "Do you suppose that I could get you to change your mind?"

Wordlessly, Hilary nodded.

"That's good," he said softly. "We'll have to see what we can do about that real soon." He brushed her lips with his. "Hilary, tomorrow you're going to paint something so good that you'll never tear it up. It will be your masterpiece—it'll win first prize at the festival." He gave her one last hug and stepped back. "See you tomorrow?"

"See you tomorrow," Hilary echoed. She was still trembling from the kiss, and for a moment after he had gone, she leaned weakly against the stair rail. Surely Jason felt the same way she did—or he wouldn't have kissed her like that. She shook her head. Was it possible that somebody like Jason, somebody so good-looking and popular, could care about *her*? Her lips were still warm from his kiss, and she put the back of her hand against her mouth to hold the warmth. Whatever happened between them in the future, this moment of their first kiss was magical, and she wanted to remember it forever.

Upstairs, the light was on in the living room. Hilary tiptoed down the hall as quietly as she could, hoping to avoid her parents. But a board squeaked, and her mother called out to her.

"Hilary, is that you? Would you come here, honey? We've got something to tell you."

Hilary sighed and went into the living room. Her father folded his paper into his lap. "Did you and Jason have a good time tonight?" he asked.

"Yes," Hilary said noncommittally. "We had fun. Jason wants me to walk up to Shell Beach with him tomorrow. OK?"

Her mother smiled happily. "Tomorrow's what we wanted to talk to you about, Hilary. Dr. Richardson has agreed to let us bring Amy home tomorrow afternoon, to spend a few days with us, and we know you'll want to be here when she arrives. Brad and Elena are coming, too, and we're going to have a little picnic out on the deck."

Hilary looked from one to the other in dismay. "But I've already told Jason—"

"I'm sure Jason will understand," Hilary's father said briskly. "Tomorrow's a big day for Amy. For all of us, really. If things go well on this short visit, she may get to come home permanently much sooner than the doctor had planned. I'm sure you want to be here to help get things started right for her."

"Yes, of course." Hilary sighed. She really

did want to be there when Amy got home, but at the same time she wanted desperately to be with Jason, and the disappointment chilled the warm recollection of his kiss.

Chapter Ten

"Of course I understand," Jason had said when Hilary called him the next morning. "Amy's homecoming is very important. Tell you what. If Sam says it's all right, I'll bring back a couple of his wood carvings so that you can work with them at home. Will you be at the shop tomorrow? How about if I bring them by the White Pelican sometime in the morning?"

"Great," Hilary agreed. "Do you really think Sam will let you have one or two?"

"I don't see why not, as long as we promise not to enter one of his pieces in the art festival without his permission." Jason chuckled. "I still haven't been able to convince him that his work is good enough to show."

"Well, thanks," Hilary replied. "I'll see you tomorrow, then." Not quite knowing how to say it, she added shyly, "I really had fun last night, Jason."

"I did, too," Jason said. She could tell from his voice that he was grinning, and after she had hung up, she sat looking at the phone for a long time, grinning, too.

Amy was coming home at three, and by that time Hilary had made a big bowl of potato salad and a dozen deviled eggs. Elena had called to say she would bring ham-and-cheese sandwiches and chips, and Mrs. Malone had made a jug of lemonade before leaving for the hospital. At about two o'clock Hilary wiped off the wooden picnic table on the deck and spread it with a yellow-checked cloth. In the middle she put a huge bouquet of wild flowers that she had gathered that morning along the lagoon. She wanted everything to be pretty and nice for Amy's homecoming.

After she had finished getting things ready, she showered, put on a clean pair of painter's pants and her pink- and white-striped blouse, and sat on the deck, watching for a glimpse of the station wagon. How would Amy feel about coming home? Wouldn't it make her unbearably sad to see her room again, to look in her closet at her white roller skates with the red pom-poms, at the delicate blue heels she had bought for the dance, and to know that there were so *many* things she would never do again? Hilary had to fight back tears. Amy had loved to skate and dance, and she had been so graceful and lovely. Hilary shook her head. It would have been better if *she'd* been the one who'd gotten hurt. She was the strong one. Maybe she'd have been able to cope with it better than Amy.

At last she saw the station wagon coming down the lane. In a few minutes her father was unloading a shiny folding wheelchair from the back and Brad was lifting Amy out of the front seat and carrying her up the stairs in his arms. Anxiously, Hilary waited at the top. Halfway up, Amy saw her and waved happily.

"Hello, Hilary," she called. "Isn't this great service? It's a lot better than riding an elevator."

"Oh, Amy, it's so good to have you home again!" Hilary exclaimed, relieved to see the bright smile on Amy's face. This time she blinked back tears of joy. Those awful hours, when they hadn't known if Amy was going to make it—they were all past, and Amy was home again!

Carrying the wheelchair, Mr. Malone followed Brad up the stairs. "This is going to be a real problem, I can see," he said, frowning.

"Once we're upstairs, there's no difficulty—the house is all one level. But getting up and down . . ." He looked over the railing. "Maybe we can rig up an elevator of some kind."

"Why don't you just wait to see how long I'm going to be in this silly contraption?" Amy asked as Brad settled her into the wheelchair. "I don't plan on being on wheels forever, you know. It might not be worth building an elevator."

Amy was wearing a pair of blue jeans, a blue plaid blouse, and sneakers, and her short, blond hair curled in a soft, shining halo around her face. *She doesn't look at all like her old self*, Hilary thought. But it wasn't Amy's new haircut or the fact that the chair she was sitting in had wheels that made her seem different. No, it was the confident, determined look on her face, a look that Hilary had glimpsed in the hospital.

Amy took in the yellow-checked tablecloth and the bowl of flowers. "Wow! A real party!" she exclaimed happily. "It's just like a birthday!" She started to wheel herself closer to look at the flowers, but Brad came up behind her and began to push the chair.

"No, Brad, let *me* do it," Amy objected. "I need to learn to get around by myself."

"Well, OK," Brad said reluctantly. "But don't tire yourself out, Amy. Remember, you've been in the hospital for a month. You don't need to do everything the first day you're home."

Amy laughed lightly. "You're just like an old mother hen, Brad," she said, teasing. "Stop fussing!"

"Hello up there," Elena called from below, getting out of her sports car. In honor of Amy's homecoming, she was dressed in a flowing white shirt made out of something crinkly and huge matching pants that seemed to billow around her as she climbed the stairs. "The sandwich lady has arrived," she announced cheerfully. "I've made a *ton*, so I sure hope everybody's hungry."

The afternoon was cool and lovely, with just a hint of a breeze off the lagoon. They had a wonderful time talking and laughing. And after they had eaten the picnic supper and Mr. and Mrs. Malone and Elena had gone inside to watch a special on TV, Brad told Amy that he had to leave early. "We're taking a charter group out to the reef for some night fishing, and I have to cut a couple of buckets of bait and get the tackle ready before the rest of them get on board." He bent over to give Amy a gentle kiss. "You'll be all right, won't you?"

"Of course," Amy said spiritedly. "Why wouldn't I be?"

Brad shrugged. "Well, have a nice evening,"

he said. "I'll come over to see you tomorrow after work, OK?"

Amy looked away. "Actually, I think I'd like to spend some time alone with my mom and dad and Hilary tomorrow evening," she said carefully. "Why don't we just skip it? After all, you've come to the hospital every single night. Maybe you'd like a couple of nights off." She laughed but there was a little catch in her voice. "I'd say you earned them."

Brad looked puzzled, but after a moment he nodded. "Well, sure, if it's OK with you." He straightened up, brightening. "Actually, there are a lot of things I've been wanting to do that I've been putting off. Mike and Joe have been planning to go fishing up at the north end of the lagoon. Maybe I'll go with them tomorrow night. And there's a surfing meet in a couple of weeks—I really need to put in some board time." He hesitated as if he weren't confident of what to say next. "Are you sure you're going to be all right? Sure you can manage without me?"

Amy nodded emphatically, but Hilary saw that her eyes were wet. "You've been marvelous, Brad. I don't know how I can ever thank you for all the things you did for me while I was in the hospital. But now I need to learn to get along without—to get along by myself."

Brad shifted from one foot to the other, and

when he spoke, Hilary could hear a note of relief in his voice. "Well, it was the least I could do, Amy, under the circumstances." He put his hand on her shoulder and looked at her for a long moment. "If you're sure this is what you really want. How about if I—give you a call in a couple of days?"

Amy smiled. "That sounds like a good idea, Brad," she said. "I hope you catch lots of fish. And tell Mike and Joe that I said hello."

After Brad had gone, Hilary turned to Amy. "What was that all about?" she asked, mystified. "Don't you want to see him anymore?"

Amy sighed and leaned back in her wheelchair. "Was it that obvious?"

"Well, it wasn't exactly obvious, but it *did* sound as if you didn't want him to plan on coming over every evening." She went to the railing and shook out the yellow tablecloth. "Does that mean that you've decided? . . ." She didn't finish the question, and for a moment there was silence.

"If you're asking whether I'm still in love with Brad," Amy said finally, "I guess the answer is no. Maybe I only *thought* I loved him in the first place." She looked out across the lagoon at a fishing boat. "What's more, I'm pretty sure that Brad doesn't really love me, either. He feels responsible for the accident and for my paralysis, and he's decided he's going to marry me and take care of me. But I don't want *anybody* to feel that they've got to take care of me!"

Brad felt responsible! Hilary dropped into the picnic bench and covered her face with her hands. Her tears came hot and fast, as if a flood had been released.

Quickly Amy wheeled over to her and put her hand on her sister's arm. "Please don't be sorry about Brad and me, Hilary. In a way, it's really a good thing that this happened, for both of us. You were right, you know, when you said that we were too young to be thinking seriously about getting married. I know that now. We both still have a lot of growing and changing to do."

Hilary wasn't listening. "Brad's wrong, Amy," she said urgently, choking back the tears. "About the accident being his fault, I mean. I wanted to tell him that before, at the hospital, but Dad cut me off. And I tried to tell *you*, but you wouldn't listen either." She looked pleadingly at Amy. "If I hadn't argued with you about riding in Brad's dune buggy, you never would have gone. I'm the one who said all those horrible things. Brad shouldn't blame himself—I'm the one who's at fault."

Amy wheeled her chair closer and put both hands on Hilary's shoulders. "That's ridiculous," she said firmly, shaking Hilary a little. "*I'm* the one who is responsible for what happened. I knew Mother didn't want me to ride in that dune buggy. You were right to remind me. But the fact that you told me not to go made absolutely no difference at all."

Hilary lifted her tear-streaked face and stared uncertainly at her sister. She remembered what Amy had said that afternoon: "I wasn't going to go. But now I will, just to show you that you can't order me around." "But you said—" she began.

"I remember what I said, and I'm sorry," Amy interrupted. "I said a lot of things that were silly and childish, especially those things about Mom and me. They weren't true. I was only trying to hurt you, Hilary. And, anyway, I just wanted to find an excuse to go. What you said didn't have anything to do with it. I went because I was being stubborn, not because anything you said *made* me go."

Hilary took a deep, ragged breath. "I wish I could believe that," she whispered.

"Look, Hilary, I can understand how you feel," Amy replied patiently. She leaned forward and wiped the tears off Hilary's face. "I bet I'd feel the same way if the situation were reversed. But I know who's reponsible, and it certainly isn't you. And it isn't Brad, either."

She smiled, and Hilary could see that new firmness around her mouth again.

Hilary felt a tremendous sense of relief. "Are you *sure*?" she asked. "If—"

"If I'd listened to you and stayed home the way I should have, none of this would have happened. So stop blaming yourself, OK?"

"OK." Hilary leaned over and gave Amy a long, hard hug. "Thank you," she whispered. "You've made me feel a hundred—no, a thousand—times better."

"That's good." Amy straightened up. "Being with you and Mom and Dad makes me feel so much better, too—and stronger. I think I can get well a whole lot faster here than at the hospital. There are so many things I want to *do*, Hilary," she burst out fiercely. "Oh, there are things I can't do right now, like roller-skating and dancing, but there are lots of things I *can* do, and that's what I want to concentrate on."

Hilary stared at her sister. She had looked at the injury in terms of what Amy couldn't do. But Amy's view was much more positive, much better. "You know, you really *do* look different," she said finally. Then she blushed, embarrassed. "I—I don't mean—that is, it's not the wheelchair or the haircut that makes you look different. It's something else, something I can't quite—"

Amy laughed. "You'd look different, too, if

you spent the whole day working out in a gym with a physical therapist and a roomful of equipment! It's great for building your biceps—I think I could lift a ton!" Proudly she flexed her arm muscle.

Hilary glanced at her curiously. "But you don't really have to spend that much time in therapy, do you? Mom said you only had to work out half a day."

"Well, if I'm going to get out of this wheelchair, I can't just sit around and twiddle my thumbs half the time, can I?" Amy demanded. "Therapy is hard work, and it takes a lot of concentration. But I really like it. In a way, it's like training for an athletic event—a race or something. Only I'm not racing, I'm just trying to get back on my feet!" She pounded the arm of her wheelchair. "And I *will* do it! I *will!*"

With a growing sense of admiration, Hilary looked at her sister. The Amy she had known before the accident had complained and grumbled about almost everything. This Amy seemed like another person. There was a maturity and cheerful determination in her voice that had never been there before. Suddenly Hilary remembered Sam's story about the tree. It had taken a catastrophe, but the Amy who had survived looked stronger and happier than the old Amy.

"But there's more to it than just the therapy, Hilary," Amy was saying. "I had a lot of time to think while I was lying in that hospital bed, and I'd like to believe I've grown up a lot. The problems you and I had before—they happened because we didn't really listen to each other. We didn't try to understand each other's problems. I want things to be different between us from now on, and I intend to do my best to make them different."

Hilary's eyes misted again, and her heart was full. "So do I, Amy," she whispered.

Amy leaned back in her wheelchair and crossed her arms. "Well, now that we've got that settled, I want to know what's happening with you. What's this about Jason Wolf? Mom told me that you two went out together last night. Is it really true? What happened to Cindy Morris? Aren't they going together anymore?"

"It's really true," Hilary said happily, relaxing a little. "We went down to the Village Pizza Parlor and had a pizza together. Cindy Morris moved away. But even before that Jason had decided to break up with her."

"You know, I really didn't believe you when you first told me about Jason," Amy admitted. "That wasn't fair of me. Are you going to see him again?"

Hilary remembered Jason's promise to bring some of Sam's carvings to the shop.

"Yes," she replied. "Probably tomorrow." She thought about his kiss and felt wonderfully happy.

"Well, how do you feel about him?" Amy asked, watching her sister closely. "Do you like him? Does he like you?"

"I like him—very much. More than I've ever liked anybody. But I'm not sure whether he feels the same way." Hilary regarded Amy thoughtfully. "You've dated a lot of different guys, Amy. How can you tell if a boy likes you?"

Amy smiled. "Well, sometimes you know right away, and sometimes it takes awhile," she said. "If he keeps on asking you out, I'd say that he's interested." She paused. "Is he going out with anybody else?"

Hilary shook her head. "No, I don't think so." The thought of Jason kissing another girl the way he had kissed her made her feel cold. "I mean, I hope not."

Amy patted her hand with a sisterly gesture. "Well, it sounds promising, anyway. I guess you'll just have to wait and see what happens, Hilary. Good luck!"

Hilary awoke the next morning with a sense of excitement and expectancy. She sat up in bed, remembering that she was going to see Jason, so she had to wear something extra nice to work. After a few minutes thought, she pulled a green print blouse out of her closet along with a pair of khaki pants and a matching green belt that emphasized her slender waist. The green in the blouse brought out the green in her eyes, and she spent an extra few minutes in front of the mirror, carefully adding eye shadow and mascara to her usual lip gloss and blusher. When she had brushed her hair, she smiled excitedly at her reflection in the mirror. Even under her own critical inspection, she looked prettier than usual, and her eyes sparkled in anticipation. Maybe Jason would even ask her to go out again that night!

For Hilary the morning dragged on endlessly. She had thought Jason would come early, certainly before eleven. But by morning's end, he still hadn't come, and she was beginning to worry. Maybe Sam hadn't been willing to let him have the carvings, she thought. Or—much worse—maybe he had forgotten about his promise. About noon Elena went out for lunch, leaving Hilary in charge, and when she got back, close to one o'clock, it was time for Hilary to go out.

"I think I'll just run next door to the deli and get something to bring back here," Hilary said, watching the shop door nervously. "That is, if you don't mind."

"No, of course not, if that's what you want to do." Elena looked at her closely. "Are you expecting someone?"

Hilary blushed. "What gave you that idea?" she asked. She had been shy about telling Elena that Jason was coming.

"Oh, just the way you kept eyeing the door," Elena said. "Let me guess. It must be Jason. Right?"

Hilary smiled self-consciously as she pulled her purse out from under the counter. "I'm expecting him to come and bring me something," she replied, and then added, "maybe."

"Well, if he comes while you're gone, I'll ask him to wait," Elena said.

The lunch-hour crowd was still lined up at the take-out counter next door, and it took Hilary nearly fifteen minutes to get her order. Carrying her sandwich and soft drink, she hurried back to the shop, hoping to find Jason waiting. Sure enough, as she came in the door, she saw him. He was standing with his back to her, beside the counter at the rear of the shop, and he had a package the size of a shoe box under his arm. Happily, eagerly, Hilary started forward. But suddenly she stopped. Next to Jason, looking cool and elegant in a white sun dress and airy straw sandals, stood Cindy Morris!

For what seemed like a lifetime, Hilary stood

frozen, staring at the two of them. Jason had just said something that Cindy obviously thought was very funny because she was laughing up at him, her eyes sparkling with pleasure. Then she casually laid a tanned hand on his arm and leaned forward very close to him. Hilary caught her breath sharply.

"Oh, Jason," Cindy was saying, "it's just wonderful to be back! I've missed everybody, but especially you. You just can't *imagine* how much!" She paused dramatically. "Have you missed me?"

Jason grinned down at her. "Why, sure I have, little lady." His drawl was like something out of an old John Wayne movie, exaggerated and playful. "I couldn't get you out of my mind."

Hilary's heart lurched painfully. She turned and left as quickly and quietly as she could, hoping no one would see her. Outside, she leaned against the wall, her breath coming in gasps. Cindy was back, and she'd made it plain that she was still interested in Jason! Maybe her family had decided not to stay in Chicago—or maybe she planned to finish out her last year of high school at Port Isabel, where she could be close to her old boyfriend.

Jason had told Hilary that he had planned to break up with Cindy even before he knew she was leaving. Didn't that make it unlikely that he would want to go back with her? But there was something else. Jason had also said that it was hard for him to tell Cindy how he felt—that her moving had solved that problem. Did that mean Cindy never found out the truth? Suppose she thought they'd get back together if she came back—and suppose Jason changed his mind. It had happened with her parents—why not with Cindy and Jason?

Hilary fought back the tears. She couldn't compete with Cindy Morris. After all, Cindy and Jason had been a couple for a very long time, and Cindy was one of the prettiest and most popular girls at Port Isabel High. Suddenly she felt sick and dizzy, and she knew she couldn't go back inside to face Jason and Cindy. She couldn't go back to work.

Blindly Hilary dropped her sandwich and soft drink into a trash can. Her stomach hurt, and eating was impossible. She got her bike and started for home, walking part of the way when she couldn't ride. Luckily the house was empty; her parents had taken Amy to the hospital for an afternoon therapy session. She called the White Pelican. "I'm sorry, Elena, but I just felt terribly sick all of a sudden," she said faintly. It sounded like a phony excuse, but it was the truth! Seeing Jason with Cindy *had* made her feel terribly sick. "I'm at home now," she continued, "and I don't think I can come back this afternoon. I hope you'll be able to manage without me."

"I'm so sorry you're sick, honey," Elena said sympathetically. "But don't worry. Business is kind of slow today. I don't think there'll be any problem." She paused and then added, "Oh, by the way, Jason came in and left a package for you."

"Was—was there anyone else with him?" Hilary asked, a feeling of hope beginning to tingle inside her. Maybe Elena would tell her that Cindy had just been shopping at the store and that Jason had met her by accident.

"A girl came in with him," Elena said almost reluctantly. "He was going to wait for you, but she seemed to be in a hurry. He said to tell you that he'd call you later about the carvings— whatever that means."

Hilary's throat felt tight, and it was hard to catch her breath. It sounded as though Cindy hadn't wasted a minute in her effort to get Jason back. "The girl—did they leave together? Did they say where they were going?"

"She said something about spending the afternoon at the pool," Elena answered softly.

Hilary could hear the sympathy in her voice, and somehow that made her feel worse. She sighed. She could just imagine how Cindy would look in a bathing suit. She had curves in all the right places, while Hilary was slim. She shook her head. It wasn't fair! Just when things were beginning to get on the right track, Cindy Morris had to come back and spoil it all!

"Oops, there's a customer coming in," Elena said hurriedly. "Listen, Hilary, I'm coming over this evening to visit with Amy. I'll be glad to bring the package Jason left, if you want me to."

"Sure," Hilary said wearily and hung up. She went to her room and stretched out on the bed, thinking of how Jason's kiss had made her feel. It *was* too good to be true, she thought, remembering how Cindy had laughed up at Jason and how he had responded to her. She lay there for a long time, staring up at the ceiling, and then she fell into a troubled sleep.

Chapter Eleven

Hilary slept fitfully most of the afternoon, unaware of her family's return. But the nap didn't make her feel any better, and when her mother called her for an early supper, she decided not to eat. Instead, she pulled on a pair of faded cutoffs and a comfortable, stretched-out T-shirt and went for a walk along the lagoon, watching the herons wading knee-deep through the shallow water and the brown pelicans teetering clumsily on the abandoned pier at the edge of the tidal flats. But the walk did nothing to dispel her unhappiness.

No matter what she looked at, Hilary kept seeing the image of Jason's affectionate smile as he gazed down at Cindy. He'd told Cindy he'd missed her—and it was bound to be true. You didn't break up with a girl you'd gone with for such a long time *without* missing her. She shivered. She had been foolish to dream that Jason could be interested in *her*, after he'd cared for Cindy.

When she got back to the house, she saw a familiar sports car parked beside her mother's station wagon, and she remembered that Elena had promised to bring her package over. Slowly she went up the stairs. She wanted to see the carvings Sam had sent, but now she could barely remember why she had wanted them in the first place. Oh, yes. She had been planning to use them in a watercolor composition, and if it was good, she might enter it in the art festival. But the festival didn't seem important any longer, and as for doing a watercolor—well, you had to *want* to paint, and she didn't really feel like doing much of anything.

"Did you have a nice walk?" Mrs. Malone asked. She and Elena were sitting with Amy on the deck, enjoying the cool evening breeze that blew off the ocean, and Hilary's father was there, too, reading. The sun was still hovering over the lagoon, but already, to the east, a full moon shone bright against the darkening sky. Amy was knitting a fluffy angora sweater. Knitting, apparently, was a skill she had learned in her first few weeks in therapy.

"It was all right," Hilary said dispiritedly. "Nothing special."

Elena was wearing leopard-spotted pants and a gauzy black top. She nodded toward a brown paper-wrapped box on the picnic table. "That's the package Jason brought into the shop for you." She glanced sharply at Hilary. "Are you feeling better?"

"I guess so." Hilary reached for the package. On the outside of it was scrawled, "Hilary—sorry to have missed you. See you soon, Jason." Her heart skipped a beat as she studied the strong, firm handwriting, and before she ripped open the wrapping, she carefully tore out the note Jason had written and thrust it into the pocket of her cutoffs.

"What's in the package?" Amy inquired, looking up from her knitting. "A present from Jason?"

A few weeks before, the hint of teasing in her words might have upset Hilary, but now it just made her feel sad.

Hilary shook her head. "He has a friend—Captain Samuel James—who does wood sculptures," she said flatly, taking off the lid. "I was planning to use one of his carvings as a model for a watercolor." She lifted the carving out. It was the graceful, one-legged heron that she had admired so much when she visited the *Princess Pat.* Carefully she held it up. The polished wood gleamed in the last rays of sunlight. "See?"

"That's beautiful," Amy said appreciatively, wheeling closer to get a better look. "He certainly does nice work."

Elena was staring at the bird Hilary held. "Let me see that," she demanded. Hilary gave it to her, and she turned the carving over in her hands, examining it closely. Then she put it on the picnic table and leaned back, looking at it through half-closed eyes. After a minute she turned to Hilary's mother. "Meg, look at the craftsmanship of this piece—the detail. Is it even half as good as I think it is?"

"It's better," Mrs. Malone acknowledged, touching the shining wood reverently. "It's simply stunning! Elena, we just have to have some of this man's work in the gallery!" She carefully handed the heron to Hilary's father. "Isn't it beautiful, Mike?"

Mr. Malone put down his book. "Very nice! Is there more where this came from?"

Elena turned to Hilary. "Where is Jason hiding this friend of his?" she asked. "Does he live here on the island? Why haven't we ever seen any of his work before? When can I see more?"

Hilary reached into the box. "I think there's

something else here," she said, fishing around in the wadded-up paper that had protected the carvings. Her fingers touched something solid, and she pulled it out. "Oh, my," she said.

In her hand she held a delicate, life-sized carving of a sandpiper. Its wings were lifted slightly, its eager head was cocked, and its beak was open. The carving was perfect, down to the last gleaming feather on the bird's wings and tail. It looked so real, Hilary could almost see it darting swiftly across the sand at Shell Beach.

Tied around the sandpiper's neck was a large tag, and written on the tag, in tiny letters, were the words: "For Hilary, who can spot a beautiful bird even when it's cooped up in a scrap of driftwood." The scrap of rough, splintery mahogany driftwood, which had once been a green tree overlooking a deserted beach, was magically transformed into a sandpiper! Looking at the beautiful carving reminded Hilary of what Sam had said about adapting to change, and as she stroked its polished wings, her sadness began to lighten.

"Sam is sort of—unusual, but he's awfully nice," she said musingly. "He lives in an old tugboat, the *Princess Pat*, in the dunes above Shell Beach. Carving is his hobby, and he has a long shelf full of pieces like this." Gently she handed Elena the sandpiper. "He carved this for me out of a piece of Honduran mahogany I found washed up on the beach."

Elena drew in her breath. "What a find!" she exclaimed excitedly. "Hilary, how soon can we arrange a one-man show in the gallery? Right after the art festival a buyer will be here to look over the works we have on display. He represents several Houston galleries, and he often buys our best pieces. I want him to see this— and everything else Captain James has." She examined the sandpiper lovingly. "I suspect this is one artist he won't be able to resist."

Hilary took back the bird, shaking her head. "I think you're out of luck, Elena. Unfortunately, Sam is kind of eccentric—and stubborn." She smiled, remembering how Sam had reacted when she had suggested that he enter his work in the art festival. "For him, carving is just a hobby. He calls it whittling, and he doesn't even consider himself an artist. In fact, he's afraid that people would laugh at him if he tried to show his work."

"Well, he's dead wrong about that," Elena said flatly. "This is the most beautiful wood sculpture I've ever seen, and I know lots of people who would agree. I'm stubborn, too, where the gallery's concerned, and I won't take no for an answer. There's got to be a way to get him to display his work." She paused, wrinkling her forehead. "You say he's a friend of Jason's? Maybe Jason can help. Would you ask him?"

At the thought of Jason, Hilary's unhappiness came surging back. "I'm not sure—" she began slowly and then stopped. She didn't want to talk to Jason—about Sam or anything else. Talking to him, seeing him again, would only remind her of how much she cared and how much it hurt to lose him—even before she'd really gotten to know him. She cleared her throat. "Anyway, I don't think it would do any good. Even talking about putting his work out where people can see it seems to upset Sam." She picked up the carvings and put them back into the box. "If you don't mind, I think I'll go to my room."

Amy wheeled her chair through the door behind Hilary. "Anything I can do?" she asked sympathetically. "You seem awfully down tonight."

"Not unless you've got a magic wand that will make an old girlfriend disappear." Hilary tried to laugh, but it didn't come out right.

"Elena told us that Jason came into the shop today with a girl. Was it Cindy Morris? Hilary, are you *sure* you know what's going on? Why don't you call Jason and ask him about it? Maybe—"

"It was Cindy," Hilary said hopelessly. "If

you could have seen how she looked at him, you'd be sure, too. And I heard him tell her he missed her. Then they went off together, to go swimming."

"Well, I still think you should find out the details before you jump to any conclusions," Amy advised. She touched Hilary's arm. "Try not to worry about it."

Hilary nodded. Amy's concern helped, even if it didn't resolve anything. She squeezed her sister's hand. "Thanks," she said.

In her room Hilary opened the box again and took out the carving of the sandpiper. She placed it on the window seat where she could see it. Looking at it reminded her of the warm sandy beach where she had found the piece of driftwood, cast up by the currents, and where the sandpiper had darted eagerly into the surf after the tiny fish. She thought of Sam's gnarled fingers, carefully cutting away the driftwood, carving and shaping and polishing it, to capture the spirit of the lively little bird—as a gift for her. Suddenly her eyes misted. Jason was important to her, more important than she could ever have guessed, and the prospect of losing him left a gaping hole in her life. But there were other important things, too, and Sam's carving reminded her of that.

The casement window was open, and the

sheer white curtains stirred in the evening breeze. The light that came into Hilary's room had a shimmering, silvery quality, and it cast a luminous glow over the little bird as it sat on the window seat. On an impulse, Hilary arranged several small shells around it, as well as a handful of dry green seaweed she had collected on the beach. For a minute she stared at the still life, the light from the window spilling over it. The scene was beautifully serene and tranquil, but there was something inexpressibly sad and *lonely* about it. It was as if the sandpiper expressed the loneliness she felt inside. Was it because the little bird was separated from all of his fellows? Was it because, for him, time stood still? Hilary hadn't felt like painting for a long time. But what was it Jason had said? "You can't put off painting until you feel good."

Hurriedly, she set up her easel in front of the window and got out her watercolors. The light wouldn't hold much longer, and she would have to work fast. Forgetting everything else, she studied the composition she had created on the window seat and then turned back to the easel, brush in hand. Painting swiftly, she finished her work in less than half an hour and stood back, studying it carefully. The watercolor perfectly captured her mood: lonely, sad, quietly reflective. But now that she had *painted* the way she felt, her feelings were under control. Yes, she was still unhappy about Jason and Cindy. But now she was calmer.

This painting was special—she was almost sure of it. But she wanted another opinion. The watercolor was still slightly damp, so she left it on the easel and went into the living room, where Elena was just getting ready to leave.

"Before you go, I'd like you to look at something," she said, leading Elena to her bedroom and pointing to the painting.

Elena took one look at it and gasped. "Hilary, it's marvelous! The quality of the light, the sheer textures, the feeling of remoteness, of—of timelessness. Did you just finish it?"

"Just this minute," Hilary answered. "Do you think it's good enough to enter in the art festival?"

"Good enough?" Elena hugged her. "Hilary, I'd be very pleased to hang your painting in the gallery, *after* it's been awarded a prize in the festival."

"Really? I thought it was good, but I didn't think—"

Elena chuckled. "Well, you *should* think," she said with a definitive gesture that made her bracelets jangle noisily. "Tell you what. I'll contribute the matting and the frame for this and anything else you want to enter in the festival. As an incentive for you and as a special thanks for your hard work the last couple of weeks. I couldn't have gotten along without you."

Hilary smiled gratefully. "Thank you," she said. "I'd like to take you up on that offer." She looked back at her new painting. It *was* good. The inspiration for it had come from Sam, from his marvelous work with the piece of mahogany driftwood. But the interpretation—that was hers. "How about if I do it tomorrow after work?" The entry deadline was only ten days away.

"Sure. I'll have to leave, but you can stay as long as you like." Elena picked up the huge leather bag that served as her purse. "When you show your friend Sam what you've done, tell him I want to have *his* work in the gallery, too." She rummaged impatiently in the bottom of her purse for her car keys. "And tell him I'm not used to being turned down, either," she added firmly as she went out the door. "He absolutely, positively *cannot* refuse. It's out of the question."

Hilary took her painting to the shop the next day, together with the six watercolors of the shells that she had done the day she and Jason had gone swimming together. The shell paintings brought back that day in crisp detail. It had been one of the happiest she'd ever known—all because of Jason. She remembered how he had kissed her on the tip of her nose when they said goodbye that afternoon. She wondered bleakly if he had kissed Cindy in that friendly, lighthearted way the day before, or whether he had held her close and kissed her lingeringly, the way he had held *her* the night they'd eaten pizza together.

Nearly every customer seemed grouchy and hard to please that morning. Twice she made careless mistakes at the cash register, and once she had to chase after a woman in order to give her the correct change. "Why don't you keep your mind on your business, young lady," the woman had chided her. But finally it was five o'clock, and the terrible day came to an end.

While Elena closed the store and rang out the register, Hilary took her watercolors to the matting table. The dominant tint in the six shell paintings was a rosy orange, so she chose a slightly textured orange mat that brought out the glowing, gemlike colors of the shells. For the sandpiper she selected an oyster white mat. A frame, she decided, even a very plain one, would distract from the quiet simplicity of the composition. Instead, she would display it, matted and unframed, between two pieces of glass.

In art class cutting mats had never been Hilary's strong point, and she had to concentrate carefully to be sure that everything was just right. She became suddenly conscious of someone rapping insistently on the window at the front of the store. "Sorry, we're closed," she called out, not looking up. But the rapping went on, and with a sigh Hilary lay down her mat knife and went to the window. Her heart rose into her mouth when she saw who it was, and her knees felt suddenly very shaky.

"Can I come in?" Jason called through the plate glass. Beside him, propped against the window, was a large black portfolio case. "We need to talk."

Hilary made herself speak, even though her lips felt so stiff she could hardly manage the words. "I don't think so," she said. "I'm busy." That day had been bad enough already. Talking to Jason would only make it worse.

"Come on, Hilary," Jason persisted. "We've got a problem to solve, and we can't do it through this window." He picked up the portfolio and stood waiting with obvious impatience. "Unlock the door."

Hilary turned the key in the lock and warily opened the door a crack. "What do you want?"

"Well, for one thing, I promised to help you

with your matting and framing," Jason said. He was smiling, but his eyes were tense and sober. He pushed the door open with his shoulder and walked into the shop. "I went to your house, and Amy said you were still at work. Then I ran into Elena, and she told me that you were matting your new watercolor. Can I take a look at it?"

Reluctantly Hilary led the way to the matting table. Why had Jason come? And what was the problem he had spoken about? He wasn't there just to help with the matting, she was sure of that.

Jason put down his portfolio and whistled reverently when he saw Hilary's sandpiper. She had finished working on it, and the simple mat set off the painting with a quiet, understated elegance. "Hilary, this is marvelous!" he exclaimed, holding it up. He glanced from it to the others on the table ready to be matted. "There's a real difference, isn't there? This has a—a greater *emotional* depth." He lay it down carefully. "Sam will be awfully pleased."

"I hope so," Hilary replied stiffly. She half turned away, gesturing to the six mats laid out on the table. "Thanks for coming, Jason, but as you can see, the mats are already cut, and I really think I can manage to finish the framing by myself."

"Seems as if I'm always interrupting you,"

he said quietly. "That first night on the dune, the day at Shell Beach, and now here." He leaned forward and kissed her softly.

Hilary stumbled back, tears stinging her eyes. "Why did you *do* that?" she whispered, her voice breaking. "Are you trying to make it harder?"

"Elena told me that you saw Cindy in here with me yesterday. Hilary, you don't understand." Jason reached for her hand.

"No, I *do* understand," Hilary pulled away. Now that Jason had forced her into this confrontation, she wanted to make it as painless for both of them as she could. "I heard Cindy tell you how much she'd missed you," she said, trying to keep her voice even. "And you said you'd missed her, too."

Jason groaned. "I was afraid of that," he said, folding his arms across his chest and leaning back against the worktable. "Listen, Hilary, you didn't hear the whole conversation. You don't know what really happened."

"I know that you and Cindy went off together for the afternoon, to go swimming," Hilary went on. She concentrated on staying calm, even though her feelings were spinning so wildly that she felt dizzy. She took a deep breath to steady herself. "Jason, I *do* understand," she repeated earnestly. "Really I do.

Now that Cindy is back, I'm sure that the two of you—"

Jason seized her shoulders with both hands. "Is that what you think?" he demanded roughly. "You think that I'm going to go back to Cindy?"

Hilary could only stare at him. The anger in his voice puzzled her. What else should she think?

Jason shook her lightly. "Couldn't you tell that Cindy was just flirting—the way she does with *every* boy—and that I was only teasing, exactly the way she expected me to?" For a minute he stared at her. Then he dropped his hands and said, almost to himself, "No, I don't suppose you could. You probably don't know what a flirt Cindy really is. And you're so serious and intense, it's probably hard for you to understand when somebody's teasing."

Flirting? Teasing? But it had *sounded* as if the two of them were serious. Listening to them, Hilary had been convinced that they both meant what they'd said. But would she really *know* whether somebody was teasing or was being serious?

"I bumped into Cindy at the drugstore yesterday, while I was on my way to see you," Jason continued. "We walked over here together, and I left your package. I'd planned to wait for you, but Cindy wanted me to go

180

over to the hotel and say hello to her parents. They're staying here for a few days while her father winds up some business. She showed me a picture of her new boyfriend back in Chicago. And then she went over to Port Isabel to go swimming with some of her friends." He paused and tipped Hilary's chin so that she had to look directly into his eyes. "I didn't go with her," he said, deliberately emphasizing every word. "I went home to finish one of the paintings I intend to enter in the festival. I thought about calling you, but I got very involved in the painting, and—" He broke off. "I didn't go with her, Hilary," he repeated firmly. "I had my mind on you all day yesterday, all yesterday evening."

Hilary stared at him. "On me?" she asked weakly.

"That's right." Jason's eyes seemed to hold her captive, and she was amazed at the intensity of his gaze. "Cindy doesn't mean anything to me, Hilary, except as an old friend— someone I once knew pretty well. Maybe it's too early to tell you this, but *you're* the one I care about."

An immense wave of happiness flooded through Hilary. "Me?" she whispered again.

"You," Jason said tenderly. "And if you hadn't been so busy worrying about your sister and her boyfriend and your mom and dad, you would have known how I felt." He stepped back, unzipped the portfolio he had brought into the store, and took out a canvas. "Here. Take a look at this. But be careful; it's still a bit sticky."

Hilary looked, but the tears that came to her eyes nearly blinded her, and she had to wipe them away before she could see clearly. The canvas was the portrait of a girl on a dune—a girl in profile, red-brown hair tangled by the breeze, standing in front of an easel, painting.

Hilary swallowed. "Jason, it's—it's wonderful," she said. "You've made me look—so different! So beautiful!"

"That's exactly the way you look when you're painting, Hilary Malone," Jason said softly. "You concentrate. You lose yourself in what you're doing. You totally ignore everything that's around you." He grinned and slipped his arm around her waist. "That's what makes it so easy to take your picture."

"You painted this from a photograph?"

"From several photographs, actually. You're just like Merriweather. You'd never hold still for me. So I took a bunch of pictures with my telephoto lens that first evening before you even knew I was there. And I took several more that day at Shell Beach. You were so intent on your work, you never even realized I was around. When I started to paint, I used details from several of the best shots." He pulled her closer, and his voice got deeper. "Hilary, I knew I wanted to paint you that first evening. And the more I wanted to paint you, the more I wanted to *hold* you. Like this."

"Oh, Jason!" Hilary's heart was so full she could hardly speak, but she didn't have to. For the next few minutes she lost herself in his kisses.

Chapter Twelve

For Hilary the next two weeks whirled by in a delightful kaleidoscope of confusion. After a week at home, Amy went back to the hospital for tests and more intensive therapy, and Hilary divided her evenings between visiting Amy and seeing Jason. Usually she and Jason walked up the beach or on the dunes, but several times they went into the village to Barney's, the hamburger joint where the kids from Port Isabel High often ate after a day at the beach. Everyone agreed that Barney's was a great place, even though it was rather dilapidated and dingy, because it was almost the only restaurant on the island where the tourists didn't go.

Hilary was very proud to be seen in Barney's

with Jason. When they walked into the pleasant gloom of the back room together, she could feel the curious eyes watching them and hear the mystified whispers speculating about Jason Wolf and Hilary Malone. It was fun, especially when Jason slipped his arm around her waist and gave her a conspiratorial wink as they found a table in the farthest, darkest corner. The second time they ate there, they chose the same table, and Hilary felt as if it were *theirs*. And when a couple that Jason knew came over and sat down with them, she felt so happy she knew she must be positively *glowing*. With Jason beside her, it seemed very easy for Hilary to laugh and tease and make small talk.

Before she knew it, too, it was time for the art festival. The three-day festival was the village's most important annual event, and everybody always got ready for it with great excitement. Wooden booths for crafts, games, and homemade foods were being erected along both sides of the main street, and the stage for the fiddle contest and the Saturday night dance band was already constructed. All the shop owners were deciding which merchandise to put out for their sidewalk sales.

But the most important part of the festival, at least as far as Hilary and Jason were concerned, was the art exhibit, which was held in the pavilion at the corner of the park. Every year the competition seemed to intensify, as more and more artists entered their work. Jason had entered his two large paintings in the oils competition—the one of Merriweather standing in the bow of Sam's boat and the portrait of Hilary. Hilary felt terribly self-conscious the first time she saw her portrait hanging where everyone could look at it. But it was such a wonderful painting that she didn't really mind very much. Jason had captured a part of her that she hadn't known existed, and when she looked at his work, she felt very proud—and very flattered. The portrait made her look *beautiful.*

Hilary had entered the set of six shell paintings under one title, *Shell Beach,* as well as the sandpiper painting, which she titled, *Still Life for Sam.*

The night before the closing date for entries, Hilary and Jason had taken a long walk on the beach. Hilary had had something on her mind for several days. "Jason," she said hesitantly, "do you suppose Sam would be awfully mad at me if I entered the sandpiper in the sculpture division?"

"I'm not sure it's the right thing to do," Jason said. "It's Sam's property, and I don't think we should enter it without asking."

"But the sandpiper really isn't Sam's property any longer," she objected. "He gave it to *me*. It's mine, and I can do what I like with it, can't I? And I would really *like* to enter it!"

"That's an argument even Sam would have to appreciate," Jason admitted after a moment's thought. "Let's do it."

On the second day of the exhibit the judges spent the entire morning making their final decisions. While they were judging, no one was allowed in the pavilion. Hilary was helping Elena in the shop that morning, and around eleven Jason walked in.

"They're ready to announce the winners over at the pavilion," he reported. "Can you come?"

"We're *both* coming," Elena said firmly. "I'll close the shop for an hour. All our customers will be there, anyway."

"I can hardly stand the suspense," Hilary moaned as she and Elena followed Jason inside the pavilion, where a large audience was gathered around a temporary stage.

Elena reached for her hand. "It won't be long now," she said. "You've waited this long, you can wait just a few minutes more, can't you?"

The master of ceremonies for the presentation was Hilary's high-school art teacher, Mrs.

Elton, who had just finished announcing the textile awards for weaving and quilting. There was scattered applause as the artists came forward to get their certificates. Ribbons would be hung on their works as soon as all the announcements were finished.

"Now we have the oils class," Mrs. Elton said, consulting her list. "I am pleased to tell you that our first prize goes to Jason Wolf for his extraordinarily fine portrait called *Girl Painting*. And an honorable mention to his second entry."

When Jason came back with his first prize certificate, Hilary flung her arms around his neck. "Oh, I'm so proud of you," she exclaimed, her eyes shining.

"It took teamwork," Jason reminded her. "If it hadn't been for you, that painting would never have existed!"

The minutes seemed to drag on, but finally Mrs. Elton got to the watercolor division. "We have an interesting situation here," she said, smiling down at Hilary, who was standing just in front of the stage. "A few minutes ago we awarded first prize in oils to Jason Wolf for his portrait of a girl at her easel. Now we are awarding first place in the watercolor division to Hilary Malone, the subject of Jason's portrait. Hilary's watercolor is entitled *Still Life for Sam*. The judges felt that Hilary's work showed a tremendous emotional depth, unusual in the work of a young artist."

Now it was Jason's turn to hug Hilary. "I told you so," he said triumphantly. Hilary stood perfectly still, hardly breathing. Was it really true? It wasn't until she held the certificate in her hand and actually saw her name written on it that she could begin to believe it.

"Now, for the last division, sculpture," Mrs. Elton said. "And again we have a very interesting situation. The winner of the watercolor competition was Hilary Malone's work called *Still Life for Sam,* organized around a wood carving of a sandpiper. The winner of the sculpture division, ladies and gentlemen, is a wood carving simply entitled *Sandpiper.* The carving itself, I understand, was Hilary's model. The artist is Captain Samuel James."

When Hilary returned from the stage with Sam's certificate, she said anxiously, "Oh, I hope Sam won't be mad at us!"

Jason looked uncertain. "Well, it's too late now. Anyway, we agreed that Sam's sandpiper belongs to you—not to him. Remember?"

"I remember, but I'm not sure now it was such a good idea," Hilary replied. "How in the world are we going to break the news to him?"

"I have a great idea!" Elena announced enthusiastically, falling into step with Jason and Hilary as they walked across the park.

"Let's all three drive out to Sam's boat. You can deliver his certificate to him in person. While you're distracting him, I can creep into his workroom and make off with a bagful of his sculptures." At the look on Jason's face, she added hastily, "Just joking."

"I think the first part of Elena's plan is a good idea," Hilary said. "I think we should drive out there, if we can all squeeze into the sports car."

"I'm game," said Elena. "And I'm willing to close the Pelican an hour early."

Jason shrugged. "Well, we'll have to tell him sooner or later. And I guess it would be better to do it sooner—before he reads about his prize in the paper. I'll meet you two back at the shop at four."

The asphalt road that stretched up the middle of the island ended a half mile before they reached Sam's turnoff, and for the rest of the way the road was a narrow, rutted track through the dunes. It was hot and muggy, and the sky looked like a piece of heavy gray slate overhead. Once in a while there was the growl of thunder. "He really came all the way out to the end of nowhere, didn't he?" Elena muttered as she steered carefully down the twisted lane to the spot where the *Princess Pat* was moored.

"I'm afraid that Sam doesn't like to entertain visitors," Jason warned. "Elena, you'd better be prepared for anything. You never can tell how Sam's going to react."

Merriweather was perched in the bow of the boat, barking madly, but when she saw Jason, she stopped barking and began to wag her tail in delight. "Hello," Jason called. "Sam, it's me. Is anybody home?"

"Howdy." Sam's face appeared over the railing, and he looked down at them. "What's this?" he asked with a frown at Elena. "A delegation?"

Jason shifted uncertainly. "Well, sort of." He glanced at Hilary as if for support. "Actually, we're a special-delivery team. We've got something for you that we hope you'll like."

Hilary held up the box she was carrying. "I've brought back the heron you lent me," she said.

Jason took a deep breath and held up the certificate. "And we've brought the first place certificate that the judges in the art festival awarded your sandpiper."

"What?" Sam's face disappeared, and in a minute he was climbing down the rope ladder. "You brought what?" he growled furiously, his gray beard twitching. "What's that you said?"

"Now, Sam, don't be mad," Jason said

cajolingly. He turned to Elena. "Oh, I forgot. Here's somebody who's really been very anxious to meet you. Sam, this is Elena. Elena runs the art gallery in the village."

"I am *delighted* to meet you, Captain James," Elena said, extending her hand. "I am really quite impressed by your work."

Pointedly, Sam ignored Elena's hand. "Well, I ain't so 'delighted' to meet you," he muttered. "Jason, what's all this here nonsense about a prize?"

Hilary stepped forward. "It was *my* idea, Sam," she confessed. "You gave the sandpiper to me, and I figured it was mine to do with as I wanted. And I wanted to enter it in the festival. Jason wasn't exactly wild about the idea—"

"But I didn't say no," Jason admitted. "Both of us are responsible. But we were right," he added hastily. "The judges thought so, anyway. They gave your work first prize."

"I see," said Sam, pulling himself up with great dignity. "Well, you folks can just turn around and git yourselves back to the south end of the island, with all them snowbirds. Somebody made a mistake, that's all. They give me somebody else's prize. I told you before—I ain't no artist. You didn't have no right to do what you did." He sniffed, then went on in an injured tone, "Jason, I would have thought better of you. Coming up here and tricking me into letting you have them pieces of whittling for Miss Hilary to use in her painting. Why, you really wanted them so you could take them down to the village where people could make fun of them—and of the old man who made them."

Suddenly thunder boomed almost overhead as if to underline Sam's point, and Hilary jumped. "But Jason didn't trick you, Sam," she insisted. "I really *did* use the carving of the sandpiper as a part of a composition. See?" Proudly she held out her own certificate. "My painting of your sandpiper won first place in the watercolor division! It's even called *Still Life for Sam.*"

Sam stared at her. "Is that right?" he muttered into his beard.

"And nobody made fun of your work, Sam," Jason added. "In fact, the judges even judged it twice. Once in the watercolor division and once in the sculpture division. They *couldn't* have made a mistake. See? Your certificate has got your name on it. Captain Samuel James."

Sam stared doubtfully at the piece of paper in his hand. "First prize?" he asked. "First prize?" There was a flash of lightning and another thunderclap, and a few huge drops of rain began to spatter in the sand.

Elena nodded, ignoring the rain. "You see, Captain James, we're all very serious about wanting you to display your carvings. It's not fair to hide your work out here where others can't enjoy it."

Sam looked at the three of them, his pale blue eyes watering. Then he looked up at the sky. "Well, now, appears like it's fixing to rain," he said mildly. "Maybe you better come down below where we can have some lemonade and talk some more."

It was still raining two hours later as they drove slowly home. Jason shook his head incredulously. "I never would have believed it," he said. "Why, I thought Sam would be furious. I figured he'd throw us out." He looked back toward the trunk, where they'd put the box of carvings Elena had helped Sam select for the show they had started to plan together. "But I think he's actually excited about having his stuff on display in the gallery!"

"Well, he ought to be," Elena said. "Only a few of the very best artists ever get a chance to exhibit their work at the White Pelican." She smiled at Hilary, sitting next to her in the front seat. "Only the very best."

Hilary stared straight ahead, hardly able to believe everything that was happening to her. It all seemed to good to be true. Having Jason for a boyfriend, winning first prize in the festival, and now, exhibiting her work at the gallery. Hilary smiled to herself. She was *so* happy.

She was still smiling when Elena dropped her off and she said goodbye and hurried up the wet stairs into the house.

"Well, *you* certainly look pleased, young lady," Hilary's father said when she came into the kitchen. He was wearing an apron, and there was a big pot of simmering tomato sauce on the stove. "It must be that first prize I heard about this afternoon." He grinned. "Congratulations, Hilary. I always figured you had it in you."

"Thank you," Hilary said modestly. She sniffed. "Mmmm. Spaghetti?" In the past weeks she and her father had grown closer, and most of her uneasiness had disappeared.

"With Mike Malone's famous homemade sauce. Want a taste?" He handed Hilary a tiny bit on a spoon, and she sipped it.

"Just the way I remember it," she said approvingly. "You used to make spaghetti sauce at least once a week when I was little."

Her father grinned and fell into an exaggerated Irish brogue. "Right you are, daughter me dear. And what's so strange about an Irishman making Italian spaghetti sauce?" He took off his apron and looked out the window.

"How about if we go for a walk? It looks as if the rain has stopped for a moment, and the sauce can simmer while we're gone."

The breeze that blew off the ocean had a sharp salt tang. Mr. Malone lifted his head, testing the air. "Feels like a front blowing in," he said as they walked along the beach on the Gulf side of the island. "We'll probably get more rain tonight." He turned to Hilary. "Now tell me why you look so happy. Your first place in the festival must be a big part of it, but it seems as if there's something more."

Hilary nodded. "Jason won a first prize for his oil painting of me, and Sam has agreed to show his wood carvings in the gallery," she said. She told her father about the trip to the *Princess Pat* and Sam's reaction to his first prize. "It was really funny," she concluded. "After he found out he'd won, he decided that his work was good enough to put in the gallery. Before that, he thought we were just humoring him."

Mr. Malone slipped his arm around her shoulders, and they walked along the sand together, matching strides. "That's what happens sometimes," he said thoughtfully. "Somebody else has to tell you you're worthwhile before you can believe it for yourself."

Hilary nodded. In a way, that's what had happened to her. Before Jason became interested in her, it was hard to believe that *any-body* would find her interesting. Knowing that Jason cared made her feel different about herself. And winning first place made a difference, too. Now she knew that other people liked her work.

"Dad," she said suddenly, "I think I'd like to be an artist when I grow up."

"You look pretty grown-up to me right now, and in two weeks you'll be seventeen," her father said with a playful grin. "And you're already an artist."

Hilary poked him. "You know what I mean," she said. "After college." At the thought of college, her stomach turned over. College meant going away from the island—and from Jason—in only one more year. But wouldn't Jason be going to college, too? Maybe, if he was willing, they could go to the same school and study art together. At that thought, she sighed happily, and her stomach calmed down. There was a whole year to get used to the idea. She didn't have to think about going away for a long while yet.

"Hilary, there's something I want to talk to you about," her father said slowly. "Your bringing up college makes me think that now is a good time to talk about it. It's about Amy—and about the family."

Hilary turned toward him. "Is Amy all right?" she asked anxiously.

Mr. Malone nodded. "Yes. They finished the last test today, and the news is very good. Dr. Richardson told us that with the right kind of therapy, Amy will be able to walk again, perhaps within the year."

Tears of happiness welled up in Hilary's eyes. "Oh, Dad," she whispered, "that *is* good news!"

"The doctor said that it was Amy's attitude that made the difference," her father continued. "If she hadn't wanted to walk again so badly and worked so hard in the very beginning, her leg muscles would have deteriorated to the point where it would never have been possible. It was Amy's refusal to give up that made it happen." He shook his head wonderingly. "You know, it's funny. I could have imagined *you* being stubborn, Hilary, and refusing to accept a doctor's opinion. But it's harder to believe that *Amy* could be so tough. I'd always thought of her as frail and delicate and—if I were being honest—a chronic complainer."

There was a sand dollar on the beach in front of Hilary, and she stooped to pick it up. "I know," she said thoughtfully, turning it over in her fingers. "The accident seems to have changed her. And I like the change." She thought of Sam's sandpiper, carved out of the mahogany driftwood. "I guess sometimes it takes a catastrophe to show us what we've got inside."

Mr. Malone nodded. "That's exactly right. And in the long run, for Amy, maybe it will be worth it. Right now, she's one tough girl." He laughed. "Have you seen her biceps lately? I sure wouldn't want to get into an argument with her!"

Hilary giggled. "Neither would I," she replied. "No more arguments!"

"Now, there's something else we have to talk about," her father said. There was a half-burned log on the sand, where someone had built a beach fire. He sat down on the uncharred end and pulled Hilary down beside him. He stared out over the water.

"Dr. Richardson said that Amy needs a different kind of therapy from what she can get at the Port Isabel hospital, Hilary. She needs therapy that's only available in Houston."

A cold shiver went down Hilary's back. "In Houston?" She clenched her fingers, and the fragile sand dollar broke into little pieces.

"Amy needs to be where she can get to the hospital every day," her father went on. "And even though I can write here on the island, I really need to be in the city, too, where I can easily meet with the people who buy my work.

I already have an apartment in Houston—one that's really big enough for all of us—so it just seems reasonable to—"

"Move to Houston?" Hilary's heart did a painful flip-flop. "But I can't!" She looked around breathlessly at the beach and the ocean. "I just *can't* leave the island!"

"But you were talking just a minute ago about going away to college," her father pointed out reasonably. "You're going to have to leave sooner or later, Hilary. You can't stay here forever."

"But college is a whole year away," Hilary replied desperately. If she left now, she might never see Jason again! It wouldn't be fair to ask him not to date anybody else during the year. And in a year's time he would probably find someone else, someone he liked as much as her. "And what about Mom?" she asked, thinking about the White Pelican. "Mom has worked so hard with the shop and the gallery, and she and Elena are just getting to be successful. You can't ask her to give it up now."

"Your mother likes the idea of moving," her father said. He picked up a stick and began aimlessly drawing designs in the sand. "Apparently she and Elena have been talking for some time about establishing a gallery in Houston, and this would give them a chance to do that. She hasn't mentioned the move to

Elena yet, but she's sure that Elena will see it as a great opportunity for the business." He turned to look at her. "You see, it all seems to be working out for everybody."

Hilary opened her fist and looked at the broken sand dollar. It *was* working out for everybody—everybody but her. "I don't want to go," she said urgently. She stood up. "I don't want to go!"

"I understand, honey. But you'll like it, once you get used to the idea. There's so much to do in the city, so much to see. And you'll be going to a much larger high school, where you can take art classes with the very best instructors. There'll be lots more opportunities for you to show your work." He looked pleadingly at her. "You'll see. It'll all work out, if you'll just try to adapt."

Adapt! There was Sam's word again! But this time, Hilary didn't feel like adapting. She didn't want to move to Houston—she wanted to stay right there on the island, with Jason, and nothing her father could say or do would ever change her mind.

Chapter Thirteen

Hilary's father had been right. The front went through that night bringing with it a chilly rain that kept up intermittently through the early morning. After breakfast Hilary made sandwiches for lunch. She and Jason had agreed to eat together down at the fishing pier. At the thought of Jason, Hilary wondered how she would tell him. What would he say?

When she was through packing the lunch, Hilary put her slicker on and got ready to.ride her bike to the shop. Her mother had already left for the hospital to pick up Amy, so her father offered to drive her to work. "It's still drizzling outside," he pointed out. "Slicker or not, you're going to get wet. Let me take you."

"No, thank you," Hilary said tonelessly, pulling the yellow hood over her head. "I'd just as soon ride my bike."

Her father studied her. "If that's what you want," he said. "But be careful. The roads will be slick." He picked up the empty bowls and cereal box and went toward the kitchen. At the door he turned. "Hilary, I know how you feel about leaving the island. But I hope you'll see it as an opportunity, not something you have to fight."

Hilary sighed. What could she say? She nodded, picked up the sack with the sandwiches, and left the house.

Riding to the village, Hilary splashed through huge puddles, hardly noticing that she got wet. Her mind was so full of what had happened the night before that there wasn't room for anything else. Her father hadn't said *when* they were moving, but since Amy's therapy was involved, Hilary supposed that the sooner the better. And, too, school would start in a few weeks, so her mother and father probably wanted to be settled into the apartment by that time.

Even the shop looked gray and gloomy, in spite of the fact that Elena had already unlocked the front door and turned on all the lights. "Good morning, Hilary!" she sang out cheerfully, heading for the gallery with a feather duster in her hand. She was wearing a red and purple smock over blue jeans, and she had an orange headband twisted around her hair.

"Good morning," Hilary said, shaking out her slicker, but she couldn't manage a smile.

Elena looked at her, startled. "Good grief, Hilary, what's the matter with you?" she asked. "You look as though you didn't sleep a wink last night."

"I didn't," Hilary admitted, reaching for the paper towels that Elena kept under the counter. There was mud on her sandals, and she began cleaning it off.

Elena looked concerned. "Is it Amy?" she asked anxiously. "Is Amy all right?"

"No, Amy's fine," Hilary turned away, swallowing her resentment. Everyone was always worried about *Amy*. Didn't anyone even care about her?

Elena put down her feather duster. "Well, what is it, then?"

"Dad says that we're moving to Houston," Hilary said flatly. She finished cleaning off one sandal and started on the other. "Amy can have some extensive therapy there. Dad can work better there. And I guess you and Mom are interested in opening a gallery there."

Elena sat down on the stool behind the counter. "We started talking about opening a shop in Houston nearly a year ago," she admitted. "But we haven't agreed on anything yet. Actually, I think it's a good thing for your mom. She's got a lot of talent for the business end of the operation. And we're almost too small here for two full-time bosses. A shop in Houston would really give her a chance to test herself." She folded her arms and leaned forward, a thoughtful look on her face. "You know, Hilary, living in Houston might be a very good thing for you, too. You're likely to have more experienced art teachers in school, and you could take private painting lessons. There's no one here for you to learn from."

"But I don't *want* to live in the city!" Hilary exclaimed, straightening up. "I want to live right here, on the island, where I can see the ocean and walk through the dunes whenever I feel like it. And I like working here at the shop, too. I've learned so much from you." Her shoulders sagged, and her voice was muffled. "And Jason's here," she said after a minute. "I don't see how I can go away from him!"

Elena looked at her closely. "How much of this is Jason?" she asked.

"A lot," Hilary admitted. More, much more than she could say.

Elena nodded. "Well, I can understand that," she said slowly. "Falling in love for the first time is a wonderful, glorious experience."

She gave Hilary a half smile. "But it's awfully painful, too. There's no getting around it. I remember that part of it pretty well myself." She put her hand over Hilary's. "I don't suppose the move makes sense to you, does it?"

Hilary shook her head, thinking about what Amy had said weeks and weeks ago. *Who cares about making sense when you're in love?* Now Hilary knew what she had meant. Now she had to admit to herself that she was in love with Jason, and she didn't really care whether staying here made sense or not. She didn't want to leave him.

Elena looked at her. "What are you going to do?"

Hilary gave a short, hopeless laugh. "Do? What can I do?" she said stiffly. "It doesn't look as though I have any choice, does it?" She felt a chill go through her, and she shivered violently. "No choice at all."

Elena stood looking at her as though she were going to say something else. But she only nodded, and after a moment she picked up her feather duster and went into the gallery.

The morning was an anguished blur for Hilary, and noon came too fast. She thought of the happiness she felt when she was with Jason. How could she give it up, now that she had found it? Would he feel the same way? Or would he feel something else? Hilary took a deep breath. Only a few short months ago, Cindy had told him that she was moving away, and he had been glad. Would he feel that way about her, too?

When Jason stopped by to pick her up for lunch, the sun was out and the puddles had vanished into the sandy soil without a trace. They rode their bicycles out to the fishing pier, which angled into the lagoon like a long wooden bridge, railed on both sides. The pier was covered with people fishing, some lines dropping straight down under the pier, where the big, clumsy sheepshead liked to shelter. Others had cast far out to the sandbars, where the speckled trout often fed.

Hilary and Jason clambered down the rocks beside the pier and found a sunny spot where they could look out over the water. Jason had brought cans of soft drinks and potato chips, and they spread their lunch out on the rock between them and began to eat. But Hilary's sandwich tasted like cardboard to her, and after a minute she put it down.

"Jason, I have to tell you something," Hilary said slowly.

"Well?" Jason opened his potato chip bag and began to munch. "Tell away."

"I—I had a talk with my dad last night. He says that Amy needs therapy that she can only get in Houston. And he and my mother both

want to move there, to my dad's apartment."
She looked out at the pier and the people fishing and the gray gulls wheeling over the blue water. A huge lump rose in her throat. "The whole family is going to move." She paused. "Right away. Before school starts."

Jason put down the potato chip bag. "Oh, *no*," he said roughly.

There was a long, tense silence. "I don't know what I should do," Hilary said finally, hopelessly. Why wasn't Jason saying anything? Didn't he *care*?

"You've got it wrong," Jason said quickly. "We don't know what *we* should do." He reached across the rock for Hilary's hand, and his eyes held hers. "This isn't a matter of 'I,' Hilary. It's a matter of 'we.' As in *us*—you and me."

Hilary swallowed. "Us?" she asked in a small voice.

"Right. Us." He held her hand harder. "Together. Jointly. Collectively. In unison." He sounded irritated. "Hilary, I don't know how to get this through your head. I care about you—very much. I'll have to admit, I don't know how we're going to handle this. But *we're* going to handle it. Somehow."

Hilary couldn't remember much of what they had said after that. They wandered for a while along the shore, talking a little but mostly just holding hands and walking, watching the wind begin to whip the lagoon into frothy waves. And then they got their bikes and rode back to the gallery.

"Let's get together tonight, after we've had a chance to think this situation over," Jason said as Hilary locked her bike in front of the shop.

Wordlessly, Hilary nodded. She didn't know what they could do. But knowing that Jason cared seemed more important than the threat of moving away, and when she went into the shop, she felt enormously better.

"I have an errand to run," Elena announced a little after four. "Will you stay until five and close up the shop for me?"

"Sure," Hilary said.

Elena took off her smock. "Feeling better?"

Hilary nodded. "A little. I had a good talk with Jason."

"Well, hang in there, kid," Elena said breezily on her way out the door. "Things will work out. They always do, you know."

Hilary gazed after Elena, trying desperately to believe in her cheerful words. Then the shop got busy, and she didn't have time to think about her troubles. At five she locked up and rode her bike home. Elena's car was in the drive, parked beside the station wagon. On the deck above, Hilary could hear Amy's light laughter and her father's deeper chuckle. As she walked up the stairs, she straightened her shoulders and tried to erase the unhappiness from her face. It was bad enough for her to be miserable—there wasn't any point in making the others unhappy, too. The decision had been made, and however she and Jason coped with it, it would be just that—coping.

Elena was sitting at the picnic table across from Hilary's mother, helping peel a basket of peaches. She looked up. "OK?" she asked.

Hilary nodded without saying anything. She went to Amy and hugged her, a little awkwardly because of the wheelchair. "I'm glad you're home again, Amy," she said, noticing that her sister looked even stronger than she had when Hilary had visited the hospital a few days before.

"Well, you'd better be," Amy answered with a wide smile. "I guess they've kicked me out of the hospital for good now, except for the therapy. You're stuck with me."

Hilary sat down beside Elena and reached for a peach. "When does your therapy in Houston start?" Her words seemed to fall into a sudden silence, as though everyone were listening.

"Whenever I can get there," Amy replied gently. "The doctors all seem to agree that the sooner I start, the better."

"Well, I guess that means the family will be moving very soon, doesn't it?" Hilary asked quietly. She bit into the peach. It was ripe and juicy, but it tasted sour to her, and she put it down on the table.

"As soon as we can," her father spoke up firmly, and Hilary's heart sank. "In fact, some people stopped by this afternoon to look at the house, and they're eager to rent it from us." He looked carefully at Hilary as if he were trying to gauge her response. "You can probably guess that we've been talking about you, Hilary. We're wondering if you feel any better about the move to Houston, now that you've had time to think about it."

Hilary glanced at her mother on the other side of the table. She was watching Hilary with an oddly hopeful half smile, and there was a misty look in her eyes.

"No, I don't feel any happier about it," Hilary said honestly, looking away from her mother. "I'd be lying if I said I did. I guess I'm just like Sam." She smiled crookedly. "I've got the beach and the dunes and the ocean inside me, somehow. I feel as though this is *my* place." She wanted to say something about Jason, too, but she suddenly felt too shy to talk about him.

Elena reached for her hand. Her fingers were slightly sticky from the peach, but they felt good over Hilary's—warm and comforting. "We've been talking about that, too."

Hilary nodded. "I know that it's good for the rest of you to move to Houston. And it's not fair for me to stand in your way." She blinked hard, trying to hold the tears back, but it wasn't any use. They streamed down her cheeks, and she pulled her hands away from Elena's to wipe them away.

Mr. Malone nodded as though he had been expecting what she'd said. "Your mom and Amy and I are all agreed that we should move." Then he added, almost regretfully, "But Elena has a different idea about what *you* could do if you wanted to."

Hilary looked up. "A different idea?"

Elena smiled slightly. "Well, you've been such a marvelous help in the shop that I've really come to depend on you a great deal," she replied. "And there's plenty of room in my house for a live-in guest." She paused and then said slowly, "If you'd like to come and live with me while you finish high school at Port Isabel, I'd love to have you, Hilary. I've never had a daughter of my own, and I'd like to have one, even if it's only for a year."

For a moment Hilary leaned back on the bench, almost dizzy with happiness and relief. She shut her eyes. Live with Elena! Stay on the island with Jason! But then her eyes flew open, and she looked anxiously at her father and mother. Would they agree?

"We're not exactly jumping up and down for joy, Hilary," her father said candidly. "It's especially hard for me to say yes, since you and I have been separated for the last year."

"And now that we're all together again," her mother added, "we'd like to *be* together as a family. For the past couple of months, I've felt closer to you than ever before." She cleared her throat. "But we also understand how you feel about leaving. And since this is your last year in high school and Elena has offered you a place to live, we've agreed that you may stay here if you want to."

Suddenly Hilary seemed to see her mother and father with new eyes. This must be as hard for them as it was for her—even harder in some ways. After such a long separation, they *wanted* everyone to be together, to be a whole family again. But they also wanted her to live her own life, in her own way. And they trusted her to be grown up enough to know what that way was.

Suddenly Hilary felt buoyantly happy, light enough to float away on the breeze. "Thank you," she whispered to Elena. "And thank you, too," she said, reaching for her mother's hand across the table. "I want to stay."

Amy wheeled around the table and put her arm over Hilary's shoulders. "Houston isn't really very far," she said sternly. "I'll expect you to come up at least once a month so you can see the terrific progress I'm making. And next year, you and I are going to take up surfboarding—together."

"It's a deal," Hilary promised, a warm tenderness rushing over her. She ran around hugging all of them. "Can I tell Jason I'm staying?" she asked eagerly.

"If that's what you've decided," her father said.

Hilary beamed. "Yes," she said simply. "That's what I've decided."

"You look a lot happier than you did at lunch," Jason said. Hilary had decided to save the good news until they were alone, and she could barely contain her excitement as they walked along the beach together, toward the dunes. "Did something happen to change everyone's plans? Have your parents decided not to move after all?" Hilary heard the hope in his voice, and it made her feel warm all over.

"Oh, Jason," she said. "The best thing has happened. The rest of the family is moving to Houston, but I get to stay! I'm going to live with Elena and help out at the Pelican and finish high school at Port Isabel and—"

"And be with me!" Jason shouted. He picked her up and spun her around, and for the first time in her life, Hilary felt delicate and light as a feather.

When Jason finally set her down, the two of them stood there, grinning at each other, and Hilary thought her heart would burst with joy.

"Oh, Hilary," Jason said, pulling her toward him. "I'm so glad you're staying." He kissed her tenderly, and as Hilary melted into his arms, the golden evening sun and the fragrant salt breeze surrounded them with happiness. And down the beach a little brown sandpiper ran lightly across the sand.

ABOUT THE AUTHOR

SUSAN BLAKE is the author of sixteen books for young adults. Her books include two others in the Sweet Dreams series, *Summer Breezes* and *The Last Word*. Ms. Blake grew up on a farm near Danville, Illinois. For over fifteen years, she has taught and held administrative positions in universities in Louisiana and Texas. In addition to her work in Young Adult literature, she has also written two textbooks and a number of articles and books about literature and the teaching of writing. She has three children and two cats and lives in Austin, Texas.

Bantam Sweet Dreams Romances
Ask your bookseller for the books you have missed

We hope you enjoyed reading this book. All the titles
currently available in the Sweet Dreams series are listed on
the next page. They are all available at your local bookshop or
newsagent, though should you find any difficulty in
obtaining the books you would like, you can order direct from
the publisher, at the address below. Also, if you would like to
know more about the series, or would simply like to tell us
what you think of the series, write to:

Kim Prior,
Sweet Dreams,
Transworld Publishers Ltd.,
61–63 Uxbridge Road,
Ealing,
London W5 5SA.

To order books, please list the title(s) you would like, and send
together with a cheque or postal order made payable to
TRANSWORLD PUBLISHERS LTD. Please allow the cost of
the book(s) plus postage and packing charges as follows:

All orders up to a total of £5.00   50p
All orders in excess of £5.00   Free

Please note that payment must be made in pounds sterling;
other currencies are unacceptable.

**(The above applies to readers in the UK and Republic of
Ireland only)**

If you live in Australia or New Zealand and would like more
information about the series, please write to:

Sally Porter,
Sweet Dreams,
Transworld Publishers (Aust) Pty Ltd.,
15–23 Helles Avenue,
Moorebank,
N.S.W. 2170,
AUSTRALIA

Kiri Martin,
Sweet Dreams,
c/o Corgi and Bantam Books New Zealand,
Cnr. Moselle and Waipareira Avenues,
Henderson,
Auckland,
NEW ZEALAND